If you love me, call me Dorrie

Bonnie Sours Smith

CHOICE BOOKS
The Best In Family Reading
P. O. Box 503
Goshen, IN 46526
♥We Welcome Your Response♥

Chariot Books

To my mother and father,
Camilla and John Sours,
who gave me the most important gift,
love

1st printing, September 1982
2nd printing, December 1982
Choice Books Edition

Special thanks to Gordon and Nancy for the typewriter, and especially to Sally for the many readings and long conversations.

IF YOU LOVE ME, CALL ME DORRIE
© 1982 Bonnie Sours Smith

Printed in the United States of America.

ISBN 0-89191-710-1
LC: 82-72710

Contents

1
Night Train
to Angell

It was very late, and Dorrie thought it must be the darkest night of the year. All the way north on the train, the girl had struggled to keep awake, fighting against the lulling sway of the cars and the comforting clacking of the wheels along the rails. It wasn't excitement that prompted her to keep her eyes open as much as uncertainty, even fear, of her destination. She peered out the window but saw only the rain and the darkness.

Dorrie curled up in her corner of the hard, slippery seat and tried to feel snug in the warm coat Great-aunt Eloise had insisted she have, "Just so those people up there know I did right by you." But inside she felt an empty coldness.

She thought about crying, but she wasn't sure how much longer it would be before the train arrived at the Angell station, and she was determined not to have tearstained cheeks and a runny nose when she was met by these new people. She was too old for that, she told herself. Eleven years old. She made it a point never to cry in front of anyone if she could help it.

They were pulling into Traverse City now. Lights glowed outside as the train slowed down and the conductor called out the name of the town. Great-aunt Eloise had told her that Traverse City was a nice town and not far from Angell, so she would at least be fairly close to civilization, even if she did have to live on a farm. Farms were frowned upon by Great-aunt Eloise.

"You know I wouldn't do this if it weren't necessary," she had said as she'd tied Dorrie's hat strings beneath her chin. With a shiver, Dorrie recalled her aunt's gaunt face with its red blotches and crooked teeth. "But, with your Uncle Albert, your mother's cousin, bless her soul, coming home from California with his wife and two children, well, there simply isn't room here for all of us. Besides, it's time they took *their* turn up north."

But Dorrie knew Great-aunt Eloise was glad to be getting rid of her. Before Great-aunt Eloise, Dorrie had stayed with Great-aunt Mary, a saintly old lady who had died peacefully one night in her sleep. And before that, Dorrie had lived with her mother's cousin Myrna, Great-aunt Eloise's daughter, who had seven children. Cousin Myrna's children had teased and tormented—frogs and butterflies and the neighbors' cats, and even Dorrie herself.

The train pulled out of the Traverse City station, out from under the lights and into the darkness again. There would be one more stop before Angell, and that was Williamsburg. The closer the train came to its final destination, the sleepier Dorrie became. She tried to picture Angell in her mind, but all she could think of was the huge Bible that Great-aunt Eloise kept on the stand in the front hall. Dorrie had opened it a few times, and had discovered a picture that showed angels,

6

white-robed and ripple-winged, flying among the clouds above a barn. Now, although she knew it was silly, she thought of Angell that way: angels above and barns below.

She must have dozed off and slept through Williamsburg. The next thing she knew, the train was slowing, and although she could see no lights, the conductor was shaking her gently. "Angell, miss. Someone's sure to be here to pick you up."

Dorrie gathered her purse and retied her hat strings under her chin. The conductor helped her down the giant steps, setting her shabby suitcase down beside her before climbing back aboard the train.

Dorrie's first bewildered glance was enough to show her that Angell didn't really have a train station. She was standing on a rough platform in a tiny valley, the only signs of life coming from the pinpricks of light in a few distant houses. She ducked her head as the wind gusted through the little valley, and wrapped her new coat more tightly around her.

The train was beginning to move slowly out of the station. It quickly picked up speed and left Dorrie standing by herself in the dark and the rain. Despite her best efforts, a few tears slid down her cheeks, but it didn't seem to matter much because of the rain, and Dorrie didn't even bother to brush them away. She wondered if anyone would come to get her.

No sooner had she wondered than she heard, above the wind's rush, the chugging of a motor, and then saw headlights coming around a corner and turning toward her. The vehicle jerked to a stop near the railway platform, and someone with a flashlight got out. Dorrie could see now that it wasn't a car after all, but a pickup truck. Great-aunt Eloise had a brand-new 1952 Studebaker, and Dorrie had never ridden in a pickup truck before. She was sure it had come for her.

"Dorothy!" called a man's voice. "Dorothy Whitfield! Are you here?''

"Here I am!" replied Dorrie.

"Dorothy?" he called again, not so loudly, and then the beam of the flashlight caught her, and she squinted her eyes.

Dorrie could see he was a large man, as he came closer, roughly dressed in a red and black plaid jacket, bib overalls, and big, mucky boots. He peered down at her, and then she could see his face, big and square, and he smiled at her.

"I'm Adam Campbell," he said. "I live across the road from your aunt. She asked me to come for you."

"I'm Dorothy Whitfield," replied Dorrie. He obviously knew who she was, but manners were manners, and she'd been taught to mind them.

Adam Campbell laughed then, a pleasant laugh. "Here we stand in the rain, exchanging names!" he said. "Come along." Picking up her suitcase, he handed her the flashlight, took her other hand in his big, rough one, and they ran to the pickup truck.

Inside the truck, it was warm, and the seat covers, unlike the hard seats of the train, were worn and soft and felt like shabby velvet, although Dorrie knew that nobody would have velvet seats in a pickup truck. As soon as the door was closed and the truck had started, Dorrie began to notice a peculiar smell, especially strong where the heater blew up from the floor. Adam Campbell's mucky boots. It was a warm, heavy, moist smell, but not altogether terrible, as she'd been led to believe. It had to be part of what Great-aunt Eloise had warned her about. She sniffed again.

Adam Campbell, as he backed the truck around and turned the corner onto the side road, noticed Dorrie's polite sniffing. "Oh," he said, "I've been up to your aunt's barn helping her deliver a calf. No time to stop and clean up—Claire just shooed me out the door, soon as she remembered what time it was. Heard the whistle blow, and she said, 'Oh, my gosh, it's Dorothy Whit-field!' Of course, it wasn't you, it was the train.'' He paused to see if Dorrie would laugh. She didn't.

She just sat curled in her corner, thinking that this place would be no different from the others. She'd been forgotten before she'd even arrived. Then the warmth of the heater and the soft seat covers became too much to resist, and Dorrie fell asleep.

Later she vaguely remembered strong arms guiding her through the wind and rain. Then she was in a place of warmth and low lights and soft voices. Gentle hands untied the hat strings beneath her chin, and her long black hair came tumbling out in a tangled heap.

Someone asked, ''Would you like something to eat, Dorothy?''

Dorrie looked up into a woman's face, noticing only her startlingly blue eyes. ''No, thank you,'' she mumbled. ''I'm not hungry.''

Then she was in her nightgown, and someone was tucking her into a big bed. The sheets were cold. She pulled her knees up to her chin, and a hot water bottle wrapped in a towel was thrust under the covers next to her cold feet. She tried to wake up enough to see where she was, to think about what was happening. But every-thing was blurred, like the view from the rain-streaked train window. Then the light was turned out.

Just before Dorrie fell asleep, she thought she heard someone whisper, ''Oh, it's just like being little again and having Margaret home.''

When Dorrie woke up, the spring sunshine was streaming in the window. *My room faces east,* she thought. *And I'm upstairs.* There was the newly leafed branch of a tree outside the window.

She liked upstairs bedrooms best. Her last bedroom had been a windowless hallway. *This is much nicer,* Dorrie thought. The walls were covered with faded pink roses. There was a white dresser, and a rocking chair with a faded, rose-colored cushion, which was much more likely to be made of worn velvet than the seat covers in the pickup. The bed she lay in was a real bed, unlike the horsehair couch in Great-aunt Eloise's hall, and had a curving white headboard and footboard. A faded patchwork quilt covered her. Through the open doorway, she could see, across the hall, the closed door to another room. She was just beginning to wonder what was behind the closed door when she heard voices coming from downstairs.

"How's the calf?" It was a man's voice.

"Fine," answered a woman. "She'll be a good milker some day."

"And the girl? Dorothy?"

"She's still asleep."

"You had quite a night of it, didn't you, Claire." Dorrie decided that voice was Adam Campbell, and he spoke gently.

"I'm just fine." That must be Aunt Claire. Dorrie imagined that the voice bristled.

She couldn't catch the words of Adam's reply. Then she heard a door swing shut. He had gone out.

The voices reminded her of the night before. The strong arms must have been Adam's, and that made her think of her father; and the clear blue eyes had been Aunt Claire's. They looked just like her mother's eyes. Dorrie wanted to cry from missing them.

It was getting a little hard to remember her mother. She had died four years ago, when Dorrie had been seven. But Dorrie could never forget the love and the sense of belonging she had felt with her. She could remember crawling into bed and cuddling up to her mother's sleeping warmth after her father had left for his early morning classes. Father had been a biology professor at the university, but that had been before mother had died. He and Dorrie had struggled on alone for a while, but then he had gotten sick with tuberculosis. Dorrie hadn't understood the disease except that it meant her father had coughed a lot. Finally, Great-aunt Eloise had come for her, and father had been taken to a special hospital called a sanitarium.

Dorrie had seen him once since then. Great-aunt Mary had taken her to see him at the sanitarium in Battle Creek. But father hadn't kissed her. "It's the tuberculosis," he'd said, with a pale smile. She didn't even know if he knew where she was now. And that thought made her runny nose snuffle even more.

No crying, she admonished herself, rubbing her eyes. After all, it was a sunny day, and perhaps they would let her see the calf.

As she dressed in her best dress, she recalled Great-aunt Eloise's admonition. "Now, Dorothy, you're likely going up there among wild and heathen folks. There's no knowing what kind of life Claire Manning might be living. It's shameful, her staying on that farm, working it like a man. Still there's no changing it—you'll have to go." Great-aunt Eloise had clucked her tongue in distress, and the rough patches on her face had reddened.

"But she's my mother's sister," Dorrie had said. "She can't be bad."

" 'Judge not lest ye be judged; vengeance is mine, saith the Lord,' " Great Aunt Eloise had quoted, her faded blue eyes narrowing.

Dorrie had turned her face away. She never argued. It wouldn't make any difference. But inside she had thought, *Great-aunt Eloise is judging.*

"You've no idea what a den of iniquity you might be walking into," her great-aunt had continued.

Dorrie didn't know exactly what a heathen was, and she'd never heard of a den of iniquity. But if Great-aunt Eloise disapproved of farms and Aunt Claire, Dorrie decided it couldn't be all that bad up north, because

11

she had learned one thing for sure about Great-aunt Eloise—she disapproved of everything that Dorrie had ever taken pleasure in. And Dorrie strongly suspected that "sin," to Great-aunt Eloise, meant going against Great-aunt Eloise's wishes.

Once she had her dress on, Dorrie stepped to the door of her bedroom and peered out into the hall. The stairway was dark and steep, and halfway down it turned a crooked corner. Dorrie tiptoed down and found herself between two rooms. One was the parlor, bright and sunny and peaceful. The other held a worn sofa and chairs and a heating stove. On either side of the stove, doors led to a tiny bedroom (Aunt Claire's, Dorrie later discovered) and a pantry. Through the warm room—and she thought of it as the warm room because of the stove—Dorrie at last found the kitchen.

Aunt Claire, dressed in blue denim pants and chambray shirt, was standing in front of the green and cream-colored wood cook stove, frying bacon. She had a mop of reddish curls tied back with a blue bandana. When she turned, Dorrie saw again those deep blue eyes, so much like her mother's. But there the resemblance ended, Dorrie thought, because her mother had had black hair, much like her own, and had been smaller, more gentle-looking. Aunt Claire looked like a farmer, tall, lean, and tanned. Dorrie's mother had always fixed her hair nicely and worn neatly pressed dresses (Dorrie remembered a pink and white seersucker pinafore). Each evening before father had come home, mother had cleaned up and put on fresh lipstick, and then dabbed perfume behind each ear and sometimes on Dorrie's nose.

"Well," said Aunt Claire, looking Dorrie up and down as well. "You ready for breakfast?"

Dorrie nodded and slid into a chair at the round oak table. A plate of bacon and eggs and toast was set in front of her.

"Strawberry jam there," said Aunt Claire, pointing with her spatula. "Last jar until berries next month." She poured a tall glass of milk from a shiny tin pail on the counter.

Dorrie's eyes widened. "Milk from a cow?"

"Fresh this morning. So are the eggs. Baked the bread yesterday."

Dorrie hesitated. Great-aunt Eloise had cautioned her about cow's milk. Then she shook herself and took a strange pleasure in drinking half the glass at once.

Aunt Claire nodded as if satisfied, and turned to the counter where a strange machine with huge silver bowls was set up. The machine began to whir as she cranked the handle. With the other hand, Aunt Claire poured part of a pail of milk into the top bowl. Dorrie stared, fascinated, as the cream and milk spurted out from separate spouts.

When Aunt Claire had finished the separating, she put the milk in the refrigerator, then took the separator apart and set it in the sink to soak. "Well, I've got work to do." She eyed Dorrie's clothes. "I didn't unpack your suitcase last night. Maybe you could do that and then change and come outside. I'll be by the barn."

Dorrie looked down at her dress, navy blue with a white collar and a red satin tie. It was her best. "Yes, ma'am," she began, but Aunt Claire was already out the door and gone.

Back upstairs, Dorrie tucked her few possessions away in the white dresser. It didn't take long. Two pairs of underwear and socks. "One on, one in the wash, one in the drawer, any more's a waste," Great-aunt Eloise had said. Plain white. Two white blouses. One shirt, one sweater, one pair of pajamas, and a second dress, a rather shabby one and getting smaller every time she wore it. It wasn't quite the thing to wear to the barn, Dorrie was sure, but it would have to do. She'd had a pair of blue jeans once—they'd been hand-me-downs from Cousin Myrna's girl Marilyn—but Dorrie had outgrown them long ago. Great-aunt Mary had never seemed to notice what she had worn. And Great-aunt Eloise hadn't held with pants for ladies. Dorrie put on the second dress, being careful not to pop the buttons or stretch the underarms too much.

All that remained in the bottom of the suitcase was a rag doll named Jeanie and a book. Jeanie had been made of red and white polka-dot fabric to begin with, but her face had faded, and her underarm seams had burst like Dorrie's dresses, and now she had pink checked patches. Dorrie knew she was too old to have dolls, but she kept Jeanie anyway.

The book was about birds. Her father had sent it to her last Christmas. Dorrie had once had more books, but they were all gone now. She didn't know where.

She set the book on the dresser top and laid Jeanie in the rocker. Quickly she made up her bed, set the empty suitcase in the closet, and hurried downstairs.

In the kitchen, Dorrie noticed that Aunt Claire had forgotten to wash the separator and the breakfast dishes, so she washed them, stacking everything neatly, and then went outside.

The screen door opened onto a small lean-to porch, which looked as if it might topple over at any minute. A well-worn path led to the barn, and Dorrie followed it past shady trees and ramshackle little sheds.

She stopped at the barn door. The sun shone on the weathered boards, no trace of red paint remaining. Looking back at the house, she realized it was almost as weathered as the barn.

Dorrie turned back and saw Aunt Claire around the side of the barn, down on her hands and knees in a patch of green vines.

"Strawberries," said Aunt Claire, as if reading Dorrie's mind. "Soon they'll be in bloom, little white flowers all over, and then we'll have berries."

14

Dorrie squatted down, studying the tight buds. She had never seen strawberry plants before. Only Cousin Myrna would have had room for plants—if she could have managed to keep all the children out of the garden, Dorrie thought wryly.

Aunt Claire glanced appraisingly at Dorrie's dress, then continued her work, tucking layers of straw beneath the vines. She did not wear gloves as Great-aunt Eloise had when digging in her flower box.

"Oh," said Aunt Claire suddenly, looking up again. "I almost forgot. The bathroom."

"The bathroom?" echoed Dorrie.

"Yes. We don't have one. That is, we have one but it's outdoors." She nodded toward a little building behind the house.

Dorrie had heard about those little buildings— outhouses, Great-aunt Eloise had called them. "I certainly hope Claire Manning has at least had the decency to put in indoor plumbing and get rid of that outhouse," she had declared.

"There's a chamber pot under your bed, but mostly I use the outhouse," continued Aunt Claire. "I guess I just haven't gotten around to fixing the house up. Rather spend the money on the cow herd."

Dorrie looked doubtfully at the little building again. It had a definite lean to it, like the kitchen porch. But if that's what there was, that's what there was. She sighed and wondered how a cow herd could be so important. Then she remembered the calf.

"Mr. Campbell said there was a calf?" she ventured.

Aunt Claire looked up. "Mr.—oh, Adam. Yes, a heifer, born last night. She's in the barn."

"May I see?" asked Dorrie.

"Sure. I'll be through mulching in a minute."

Dorrie stepped inside the barn. It was filled with pleasant smells and dusty shafts of sunshine. She heard rustling sounds and, walking further in, saw a huge

15

brown and white cow. The cow turned her head toward Dorrie, wisps of hay hanging out each side of her mouth as she chewed. She rolled her great brown eyes and mooed. The low, echoey sound startled Dorrie. She was glad to see the rope tied securely around the cow's thick neck, and she wondered where the calf might be. Suddenly the cow swung her head around and nudged something on the floor at her side, and there, nestled in a bed of straw, lay the calf. Its mother's nose must have awakened it, for it struggled to its feet and stood staring at Dorrie. It was the leggiest, wobbliest creature Dorrie had ever seen.

"Cute, huh?" said a voice behind her. It was Aunt Claire.

"She's beautiful," whispered Dorrie.

"You can pet her," said Aunt Claire.

Dorrie hesitated, not wanting to miss this chance, but not sure what the mother might do.

Aunt Claire reached over and patted the big cow's nose. "Some cows are fussy, but not Bluebell."

"Bluebell?" Dorrie thought it was a lovely name.

"Some farmers give their cows numbers, but I still like names." Then Aunt Claire said, "Come pet the calf and think of a good name for her."

Dorrie tiptoed over to the calf and reached down to touch her nose. "Wet!" she exclaimed, in surpirse, but she didn't take her hand away.

The calf stretched out its long pink tongue and licked Dorrie's hand. "Oh, it's rough—like sandpaper."

Aunt Claire smiled. "Think of a name yet?"

Dorrie ran her hand down the calf's silky back. "Oh, no, I couldn't. She's not mine," said Dorrie.

"But you live here," said Aunt Claire.

"I'd only have to leave her," replied Dorrie in what she hoped was a matter-of-fact voice. "I never seem to stay very long."

Aunt Claire said nothing.

16

2
Ghosts and Blue Jeans

The next day was Sunday. Dorrie came downstairs in her second dress. She was sure Aunt Claire didn't go to church. Great-aunt Eloise had taken care to emphasize Aunt Claire's un-Christian qualities, such as farming and lack of indoor plumbing. Much to Dorrie's surprise, Aunt Claire stood at the green enamel stove, not in her denim pants and work shirt, but in a dress. It wasn't much of a dress, thought Dorrie. No lace, no flowers, no bright colors. *Like my clothes,* she thought, *only Great-aunt Eloise doesn't pick Aunt Claire's.* The chestnut red hair was combed and tied back with a ribbon.

Aunt Claire turned when Dorrie came in, her eyes glancing over the dress. "This morning you can put on the other one," she said.

Great-aunt Eloise had always taken Dorrie to the big stone church four blocks from their house. Inside it had been dim and gray. The minister had stood so far away that Dorrie would never have been able to recognize him later if it weren't for the fact that he called on Great-aunt Eloise once a month to discuss the finances of the Ladies Aid Society. The stained glass windows had fascinated Dorrie, and each Sunday she had spent the hour studying the gentle face of a man with a lamb in his arms.

It came as a shock to Dorrie, when they arrived at Aunt Claire's church, to find, not a gray stone cathedral, but a little white clapboard chapel with a simple steeple, all sadly in need of paint and looking as common as a house. The sign beside the open door read: Angell Church. The windows were tall and rounded at the top, and of clear glass, all except for one. And that one was stained glass—a picture of a man carrying a lamb. It was a simpler picture than the other one, more like a picture in a coloring book, but it was the same man. Dorrie smiled at him.

After church, Aunt Claire introduced Dorrie to the minister. "Pastor, this is my niece, Dorothy Whitfield. Dorothy, this is Pastor Linden."

The pastor shook Dorrie's hand and smiled down at her. He was blond and young and tanned, and he had the same gentle eyes as the man in the window. "Margaret's girl, I can tell," he said.

Dorrie looked from him to Aunt Claire. How did he know her?

"I'll have to come visit both of you soon, Claire," Pastor Linden continued. "Maybe you'll fix us some of your special homemade ice cream." He winked at Dorrie, and she smiled back.

"Why, Claire Manning," a booming voice behind them interrupted. "What have you here!"

Dorrie turned around to see what she thought must be the largest woman in the world approaching. She rushed upon them from across the churchyard, her huge hips rolling, and for a minute Dorrie was afraid she would laugh, because the woman moved so much like Bluebell. She had rosy cheeks and piles of yellow hair pinned up on top of her head, crowned by a ridiculously tiny white hat with a wispy veil.

"Hello, Ida," said Aunt Claire, with a sigh.

"Why, Claire Manning, what have you here?" the woman repeated.

"Ida, this is my niece, Dorothy Whitfield. Dorothy, this is a neighbor of ours, Miss Crawford."

"Why, I didn't know you were expecting company this weekend, Claire-dear," continued Miss Ida Crawford, beaming down at Dorrie.

"I'm not, exactly," said Aunt Claire. "Dorothy is staying with me—for a while."

Miss Crawford's eyebrows shot up. "Oh, a little vacation."

"No, well, I suppose. . . ."

"Margaret's daughter, isn't she? Well, how is that handsome professor father of yours, my dear?"

"Fine, ma'am," replied Dorrie as politely as she could.

"Well, I certainly must come up to visit one of these days, us being such close neighbors and all," declared Miss Crawford. A horn tooted. "Oh, there're the Willises calling," she said. "Can't miss my ride." And with a wave of her pudgy, gloved hand, she waddled off to the car. Dorrie watched, fascinated. When Miss Crawford climbed into the car, one whole side of it sank, and it drove away with a decidedly lopsided look.

She looked back at her aunt for a trace of a smile, but found none.

"Come along, Dorothy," said Aunt Claire. "I think that's enough for one day."

After the dinner dishes were done, Dorrie sat in the porch swing, thinking about the fact that Aunt Claire hadn't told Miss Crawford she was staying here. Perhaps she wasn't staying. Perhaps it was just a vacation, and Aunt Claire would send her on to someone else, though Dorrie couldn't imagine who. *And perhaps it really doesn't matter to anyone where I am,* thought Dorrie.

Just then she heard singing. "When the roll is called up yon—der," came the deep booming voice, and Dorrie looked up to see Adam striding purposefully across the shady lawn. His driveway turned off the dirt road just across from their own and curved back into his orchard. From where she sat, Dorrie could barely see his house, a small, unpainted building, little more than a shed, hidden among the trees.

Adam saw her and waved. "Any pie left?" he called. He lifted himself up onto the porch railing and sat among the potted geraniums. "Well, how are you getting along here, Dorothy Whitfield? That is your name, isn't it?" His blue eyes twinkled.

Dorrie nodded. Was he teasing her? No one had ever really teased her, except mother. "Yes. But you can call me Dorrie."

"I can? And why is that?"

"My mother always called me Dorrie," she explained.

He gazed into her solemn eyes. "Then I will call you Dorrie too."

"Did you know my mother? People at church did. Even Pastor Linden. But he's too young to have been the pastor when my mother was a little girl, isn't he?"

Adam laughed. "You're right. Much too young. As a matter of fact, Matthew Linden and your mother Margaret, and Claire were all in Sunday school class together. Me too."

Dorrie's eyes widened. This was incredible. "You, too? All of you?"

"Well, I wasn't actually there all the time. There's a creek behind the church, down in the woods. On summer Sundays I'd sneak away from my folks and go looking for fish or tadpoles or birds' nests. I guess I was a bit of a disappointment to my Sunday school teacher."

"My father likes tadpoles and birds' nests too," Dorrie observed.

"You father's a fine man. You must miss him."

Dorrie nodded. It felt good to be talking to someone about her mother and father. Great-aunt Eloise hadn't been much of a listener, and Aunt Claire had not even mentioned Dorrie's parents so far. "My father's in a sanitarium now, so that's why I'm . . . here."

"Yes," said Adam.

"How did you know?" asked Dorrie, amazed by how many people in Angell seemed to know her life story when she hadn't even met them until two days ago.

"Oh, word gets around. Your Aunt Claire told me."

"My father wasn't from around here, was he? Just mother?"

"Oliver, your father, that is, was from downstate. You've heard the story of how they met, haven't you?" asked Adam.

"Yes, I think so," Dorrie hedged. "But . . . it's been so long."

"Well, I'll tell you," said Adam, leaning back against a porch post and folding his arms. Dorrie decided to sit beside him, moving a geranium pot to make more room.

"It was about this time of year," began Adam. "It was your mother's graduation night, and when Oliver Whitfield walked into the school, well, your mother began turning all shades of red. Said she wasn't going up on stage with the rest of the class to get her diploma, said maybe she'd faint, thought she should go home. And none of us knew what was the matter." Adam stopped.

Dorrie's eyes brightened. "What *was* the matter?"

Adam continued with a grin. "It seems that that

morning, your mother had gone down to the creek in the back pasture. She had on her old gardening clothes, and her hair was all done up. Not done up fancy, but getting curled. You know?''

Dorrie nodded. "Done up in rags," she said, remembering. "It looks an awful mess until you take it out."

Adam laughed. "That's it. She looked an awful mess. She was walking across the creek on that log bridge when something in the willows startled her. She said later she thought it was the bull, and your mother was scared to death of that bull. Well, the next thing she knew, she was sitting on that creek bottom, spitting and sputtering, soaking wet, curls and all. And what should come into view? Not that bull, no, sir. Oliver Whitfield and a butterfly net!''

Dorrie giggled. "Oh, no!''

"Oh, yes!" Adam continued. " 'I hope you realize you have just caused me to lose the best specimen I have seen so far because of all your splashing and caterwauling,' says your father. 'Me?' shouts Margaret. 'Just look at what you've done to me! Look at my curls—no, don't look at my curls!' ''

Dorrie began to laugh at Adam's high-pitched imitation of her mother's voice. "What was my father doing here?" she asked.

"Oliver had just finished his first year of teaching at a big university downstate—he was a good deal older than your mother—and he was on what he called a field trip. Came up north to get specimens for his classes. He was boarding down the road at Crawfords'.''

"Not Miss Ida's?" cried Dorrie.

"That's the place," said Adam, with a chuckle. "Suppose you met her at church this morning. Feed folks real good down there at Crawfords', don't they?''

As Dorrie giggled again, a potted geranium teetered on the railing beside her and then plopped into her lap.

22

"What's going on out here?" It was Aunt Claire at the screen door.

"Come on out, Claire," said Adam, catching the pot before it hit the floor. "We're just spending a quiet Sunday afternoon on the porch." He winked at Dorrie.

Dorrie brushed the loose dirt off her dress.

"Oh, Dorothy, your dress," scolded Aunt Claire, coming out on the porch. "What were you doing?"

"I don't know why you haven't got her into blue jeans anyway, Claire." Adam set the geranium back on the railing.

"She hasn't any," Aunt Claire retorted.

"Now, Claire," soothed Adam. "We were just sitting here, talking about how her folks met, and how embarrassed Margaret was at graduation when Oliver walked in." He chuckled again. "Remember how red her face got, Claire? And how we all laughed when she told us the story?"

Aunt Claire's face softened. "Yes, I remember. Now, Dorothy, let's see that dress. And you'd better go wash those hands."

Dorrie looked over to Adam and he nodded. "Run along, Dorrie," he said. "Get washed up, and maybe we can have some pie in a bit."

Dorrie went inside, lingering in the warm room where she could still hear them talking.

"What's this 'Dorrie' business?" Aunt Claire was saying.

"That's her name, which you would know if you took some time with her."

"What's that supposed to mean? I'm to sit around all day making her feel bad by bringing up ghosts from the past—by talking about a mother who's dead and a father who's got tuberculosis?"

"Feel bad?" echoed Adam. "Claire, you've got no idea what that girl needs, how she feels. She's lost so much that . . ."

"I know what losing feels like." Aunt Claire's voice rose. "Mama and papa in one winter. And—and Margaret. Now, sooner or later somebody else will come get Dorothy, and when that happens, well, I just don't plan on breaking my heart over her."

"Claire," said Adam. "Oh, Claire, if you would just—"

"Hush," scolded Aunt Claire, and the voices faded.

Dorrie went on into the kitchen and turned the faucet on full blast.

The next week the apple trees bloomed in Adam's orchards. The air was full of the fragrance of the delicate blossoms, pale pink and looking like paintings on china plates. And Dorrie thought she felt like the blossoms, unfolding from the tight bud that she was, from the closed-up feeling she'd had at Great-aunt Eloise's.

Since there had been only two weeks of school left when Dorrie arrived, Aunt Claire had decided that she didn't have to go. And one morning Adam came and took her to Angell instead. "Going shopping" was all he would say as he parked in front of the only store.

"Angell General" read the lopsided sign over the door. Inside the dimly lit store were shelves of calico bolts and eyelet lace. From the beams hung red lanterns and leather boots. There was a counter with neetsfoot oil and saddle soap and cucumber soaps for ladies' complexions. Up front, Dorrie saw molasses and dried beans and tins of meat. Pairs of red suspenders hung from a nail in a post. In the window were glass jars full of candies.

A big potbellied stove stood in the center of the store with several chairs gathered around it. A fat little man with a bald head and bushy eyebrows sat in a rocker, his feet propped up on the stove railing. He had nodded good morning to Adam when they'd come in, but while Dorrie looked around he had continued reading his newspaper and made no attempt at conversation. Now he looked up.

"Finding everything, Adam?" he inquired.

"Yep," replied Adam, picking a can off a shelf and filling a brown paper bag with crackers from a barrel. "Just point us to the girls' blue jeans, Jesse."

"Boys, girls, all the same," said the proprietor, jerking his bald head in the direction of a far counter. "Over by the baking soda."

"How do you keep track of everything?" Dorrie asked.

"Easy," answered Jesse. "Alphabetical order."

"Like gingersnaps next to jawbreakers?" said Adam, winking at Dorrie.

"That's right."

"Then how come you always keep the sardines by the dental floss?" Adam wanted to know.

"Sardines? They're under *D*—for dead fish."

Adam had a mild choking spell, and Dorrie buried her face in a stack of blue jeans to keep from laughing out loud.

Then Adam sorted through the blue jeans and held a few pairs up to Dorrie's waist to measure. "Here," he said at last, thrusting a pair at her. "Go behind that curtain there and try them on."

Dorrie couldn't remember trying on clothes at a store before, and her hands trembled with excitement as she hoisted up her dress to pull the blue jeans on over her thin white legs.

"Well, how do they fit?" called Adam.

"A little long. A little too big, maybe. But, oh, they're wonderful!" The pants were stiff, and she felt awkward, but it was a good feeling. She stepped around the curtain for Adam to see.

"They'll do," he said. "You need growing room for the summer." Then he looked again. "Have you got a shirt?"

25

"Blouse," corrected Dorrie. "Boys wear shirts. I have two white blouses. One for good and one for . . . not so good."

"Not so good?" echoed Adam.

"Well, it's older and smaller."

"Jesse, where're the shirts? Under *S*?"

"*F* for flannel mostly," Jesse called back. "A few more under *S* for short sleeves."

Adam shook his head and found a stack of cotton shirts. They searched for Dorrie's size and found three—a navy blue, a dark green stripe, and a red plaid. "Sorry, Dorrie. There's nothing fancy here for girls. Take your pick."

Great-aunt Eloise would have chosen the blue, unless she'd been in an exceptionally good mood. Then perhaps she might have allowed Dorrie the dark green stripe. Dorrie quickly picked up the bright red plaid and looked up at Adam for approval.

Adam smiled. "I think you picked the best one. Now go put it on. Here's a sack for your dress and slip."

"She need any shoes? Got boots and tenny-shoes," said Jesse from his rocker.

"No," replied Adam, laying a few dollar bills on the counter. "She's going barefoot this summer."

Dorrie grinned from behind the curtain.

"Let's go, Dorrie," said Adam. "See you later, Jesse."

Jesse waved his hand and returned to his paper. He had never once gotten out of the rocker or taken his feet off the stove railing.

Out in the pickup, Adam opened the paper bag he carried. "Snack time," he announced.

"Snack time?"

"Sure. You're hungry, aren't you?"

Dorrie nodded.

"Of course," Adam went on. "And I'm always

hungry." Opening the paper bag, he brought out a handful of crackers for each of them and a tin of sardines to share. "You ever had sardines before?"

Dorrie shook her head. "Dead fish, he called them."

"Dead fish they are!" agreed Adam, laughing.

"But how do you get in?" asked Dorrie.

"Oh, you mean into the can? Watch." Adam produced a little key from the underside of the tin. He fit it to a metal strip and began winding the lid up into a long roll.

Dorrie watched as the lid wound up, revealing neatly stacked little fish in oil. She wrinkled her nose at the smell. Adam used his jackknife to unwedge a fish, and laid it on a cracker for her. Cautiously Dorrie took a bite, the cracker crumbling in her hand.

A pretty delicious little dead fish, she had to admit as she chewed it up. She grinned and reached out for another one. Adam smiled in satisfaction.

When they arrived home, they found a strange car in the drive. Frowning, Adam swung the pickup wide around it.

"Who's here?" asked Dorrie, brushing cracker crumbs from the front of her new shirt.

"Preacher," said Adam, a little gruffly, Dorrie noticed.

But she didn't stop to think about his tone of voice. "Pastor Linden!" She opened her door and ran to the house, Adam following slowly.

Aunt Claire was standing on the front porch, holding an armful of books and papers. Beside her stood Pastor Linden, hat in hand, smiling the same smile that Dorrie remembered from last Sunday.

"Here she comes," he said, as Dorrie bounded up the porch steps and then came to an abrupt halt, suddenly shy and embarrassed.

Dorrie nodded her head politely. "Pastor."

"I've just persuaded your aunt to take over the older

girls at Sunday school. That would be your class, Dorothy.''

My class, she thought. She'd never been to Sunday school before. Great-aunt Eloise had said it meant getting up too early, and had muttered about stories, games, and crafts. To Dorrie it sounded like fun and, possibly, new friends.

"Hello, Adam," said Pastor Linden as Adam approached. They shook hands, and then Adam stuffed his fists in his pockets. "I was just telling Dorothy that Claire has consented to join our Sunday School staff.''

Dorrie thought Adam looked surprised. He stared at Aunt Claire, his mouth dropping open slightly.

"Well, I—'' began Aunt Claire. "You see—''

"No, I don't see," said Adam.

"Well, Halley Burton's had that class for two years, since before she got married, and now their baby's due this summer, and well, I'm just going to fill in for a while, Adam. It's only temporary. Just until the baby comes and Halley's on her feet again.''

Adam shook his head. "What time are you planning to get up on Sundays to do your chores, Claire Manning? Pitch dark?''

"I can manage just fine, thank you," she retorted.

"Well, just don't expect me to come trotting over on Sunday mornings to help get them done in time!" And he turned and stomped down the porch steps and off across the yard toward his own house.

"He forgot his truck," whispered Pastor Linden in disbelief as they watched him go. "He just walked off and forgot his own truck.''

Aunt Claire sighed. "Oh, you know Adam, Matt. He'll remember where he left it in a day or two.''

"Yes. Well, I suppose I should get along. I want to stop off at Burtons' and tell Halley. I really do appreciate it, Claire. I'm sure—well, I think you'll grow to enjoy it.''

Aunt Claire smiled weakly.

They stood silently on the porch, watching as Pastor Linden drove away. Dorrie thought Aunt Claire seemed tired. Her shoulders were drooping, and her face didn't look happy.

"I'll help you, Aunt Claire," she offered gently.

"What?" Aunt Claire turned. "What did you say?"

"I said I'd help you. With the Sunday morning chores. So we can get to Sunday school on time. I'll even help you every morning," she went on. "I'm strong. I used to work for Great-aunt Eloise. I can help you do chores."

Aunt Claire began to smile. Then she bent down, looking at Dorrie closely. "Why, Dorothy, where did these clothes come from? And what do I smell! Fish?"

"Dead fish," explained Dorrie. "Adam took me to the Angell General Store."

"He bought you a shirt and blue jeans, and I bet he bought some crackers and a tin of sardines, didn't he?" Aunt Claire straightened the collar of the red plaid shirt, and a few more cracker crumbs rolled out.

"Sardines," repeated Dorrie. "Only Jesse called them dead fish! We didn't have too many. It didn't spoil my appetite, honest."

"No, I don't suppose it did. And you and Adam had a good time?"

Dorrie's eyes shone. "Oh, the best. Nobody ever took me shopping like that before. And look—" She pulled at the front of her shirt. "It's red! I got to pick it out myself!"

"Oh, Dorothy," sighed Aunt Claire, "I—" She stopped abruptly.

"What?" asked Dorrie after a moment, trying to probe her aunt's faraway blue eyes.

But Aunt Claire shook her head and smiled. "Oh, nothing, Dorothy." And the faraway expression was gone.

3
Mystery
in the Attic

June came, and with it came summer. On the first Sunday of the month, Aunt Claire got up an hour earlier than usual and called to Dorrie from the bottom of the stairs. Dorrie heard her voice from far away, as if in a dream.

"It's Sunday morning, Dorothy. Do you still want to help with chores?"

Then Dorrie remembered. The Sunday school class. She opened her eyes and looked around the now familiar bedroom, with its faded roses on the walls. Early morning light was creeping in the east window. "Coming, Aunt Claire," she called.

She couldn't remember ever having been up quite so early. The surrounding valleys and orchards were wrapped in fog. Only their hill farm and the tops of neighboring hills held their heads up, and it seemed to Dorrie like being on an island in a misty sea, looking across at other islands and wondering if there was anyone on them looking back at her.

"Will the cows be surprised to see us an hour early?" asked Dorrie, on the way to the barn.

Aunt Claire laughed. "I don't think they can tell time. But maybe they can sense we're early today."

The cows mooed their greetings, and Dorrie patted each one and called it by name. "Parsnip and Clover and Bluebell and Snapdragon and Marjoram. Aunt Claire, what's Marjoram named for?"

Aunt Claire pitched down another forkful of hay. "It's an herb from the garden. I use it in meat loaf and soups."

"I like that name. How do you know to pick names like that?" asked Dorrie.

A voice from the doorway answered quietly, "Because she's just that kind of woman."

"Adam!" exclaimed Aunt Claire. "What are you—"

"Doing here?" he asked. "It's the Lord's day, Claire. I may not show up at church more than once or twice a year, when the Spirit moves me. You know I don't care for the mirror worshippers. But I couldn't sit home, knowing you were working extra hard to get to Sunday school, and not come help."

"Mirror worshippers?" echoed Dorothy.

"Dorothy, you can feed the chickens," said Aunt Claire. "Feed's there by the door. You've watched me scatter it and put extra in the chicks' pans."

"Claire, are you ignoring me?" asked Adam. Dorrie stopped halfway to the door, between Adam and Aunt Claire.

Aunt Claire sighed. "No, Adam. I'd like to think I didn't need help. But I do—thanks."

A big grin spread across his face. "Then get yourself down from there, Claire Manning," he said. "You milk, I'll pitch hay."

The chores were soon done. Aunt Claire showed Dorrie how to shoo the hens off their nests and gather the eggs, big, brown, and warm. And she promised to teach her to milk Bluebell.

Adam had a cup of coffee while Aunt Claire mixed up fresh buttermilk pancakes, and Dorrie took a much-needed bath in the clawfoot tub.

"If only Great-aunt Eloise could smell me now!" Dorrie grinned to herself before climbing in.

After she and Aunt Claire were dressed in their Sunday clothes and breakfast was over, Aunt Claire gathered up her worn Bible and the extra books Pastor Linden had given her. "Thanks again for helping," she said to Adam on the kitchen porch.

"Sure, Claire," he replied with a smile. "When I teach a Sunday school class, you can come over early and help me spray orchards or pick apples."

"Oh, Adam," scolded Aunt Claire. But Dorrie noticed that her cheeks reddened, and that she turned to hide her smile from Adam. "Come along, Dorothy, or we'll be late after all."

"Watch out for fog in the valley," Adam called after them.

As they backed out of the driveway, Dorrie watched Adam, still standing on the porch, waving good-bye to them.

"He looks as if he belongs there."

"What?" asked Aunt Claire.

"I said Adam looks as if he belongs there."

Aunt Claire's secret smile was gone again. "Where that man really belongs is in church," she said, sounding irritated.

"Then why isn't he coming with us?" Dorrie asked. "And what did he mean about mirror worship?

"You'll have to ask Adam to explain those questions," was all Aunt Claire would say.

Dorrie sighed. "Well, anyway, he still looks like he

belongs. Not like he's neighbors. More like he's family.''

Aunt Claire gave her a strange look and then laughed. But Dorrie didn't notice, because she was just beginning to realize that Adam was the first person to feel like family to her since mother had died and father had gone away.

In church, Dorrie whiled away the time by watching the big rose on the organist's hat bobble up and down. She watched other girls make fans of their bulletins, just like the old ladies did. She looked at the hymnal and read the wedding vows and the burial rites in the back. And then suddenly she felt warm all over, and looking up, she saw the sun streaming in the shepherd window. The pastor's voice faded away as Dorrie sat in her pool of sunshine, transfixed by the brilliance of the lighted colors in the stained glass. The shepherd was no longer a picture in a coloring book, but a person. He was real.

When they came out of church, the fog had completely disappeared, retreating to the hidden valleys it had sprung from, and the green leaves were a translucent gold in their newness.

Once home, Dorrie set the table while Aunt Claire stirred up milk gravy on the stove.

''The shepherd,'' said Dorrie. ''Who is the shepherd?''

Aunt Claire glanced up, puzzled. ''What shepherd?''

''The one in the window at church.''

''Oh, the shepherd,'' said Aunt Claire, as if there were only one in the whole world. ''That's Jesus. The Good Shepherd.''

''Was Jesus really a shepherd?''

''No, he was a carpenter.''

''Then how come the window is of a shepherd?

Great-aunt Eloise's church had a shepherd too.''

Aunt Claire stiffened a moment, then smiled and stirred rhythmically. ''Jesus did call himself that once. And in the Psalms, it says, 'The Lord is my shepherd, I shall not want.' ''

Dorrie giggled. ''Are we sheep, then?''

'' 'We are his people, the sheep of his pasture,' '' Aunt Claire answered. ''That's another psalm.''

Dorrie stared. ''I'm a sheep? Not really.''

Aunt Claire laughed as she poured the gravy out, smooth and steaming. ''You are his lamb, Dorothy. As surely as if he'd made you with four legs and a woolly coat. Does that sound strange to you? It's poetic, a comparison.''

Dorrie was warmed by the thought of being a lamb like the one the shepherd held close in his arms. Of being in Jesus' care just as the lamb was in the shepherd's. She squinted up at Aunt Claire. ''The window,'' she said. ''This morning, when the sun began to shine, it made the glass look like jewels. It turned the shepherd from a picture into a person.''

''Yes. I saw it too,'' replied Aunt Claire. ''God is the sunshine, and we are his stained glass windows. He wants his love to shine through us.''

Dorrie's laughter rippled through the kitchen. ''I thought we were his sheep.''

''We are a lot of things to him. The Good Shepherd died for his sheep because he loved them.''

''You mean the cross? I know about the cross.''

Aunt Claire slid the juicy roast from the pan to the platter. ''Yes. He wanted to save us. And because he died, we can spend forever with him in heaven, if we believe.''

''Do you believe it's real?'' asked Dorrie. ''Is heaven real? And is mother there?''

''Yes, oh, yes, it's real. And your mother is there.''

''What's it like there, do you suppose?'' Dorrie

slipped into her chair and spread her napkin on her lap.

"Heaven," sighed Aunt Claire. "Maybe it's a little bit different for different people. For me, it's sunny meadows and a grape arbor and fellowship suppers every night—and Brown Swiss cows."

"Brown Swiss cows?" echoed Dorrie.

Aunt Claire grinned. "I can't afford them now. I figure maybe I can have some in heaven."

Dorrie was quiet for a moment. At last she sighed and said, "In heaven there's a rocking chair and books to read and mother's lap to sit on."

After dinner, Adam came over for rhubarb pie, and the three of them sat on the front porch. Adam read the Sunday paper, and Aunt Claire worked on the quilt for Halley Burton's baby, and Dorrie just sat on the wicker sofa. It was very warm and pleasant, and Dorrie listened to the lullaby humming of Aunt Claire's voice and the creaking of Adam's rocker and the droning of the bees in the hollyhocks, and soon she fell asleep.

After that Sunday, Dorrie got up early every morning to help with chores. Often, Adam came by to help finish up and then to have coffee or breakfast, though he never went to church afterwards. Dorrie quickly grew to love those early morning times. The welcoming sound of the cows and chickens, the smell of hay and grains, the feeling of being needed and depended upon. Aunt Claire began teaching Dorrie to milk Bluebell. And the calf in the pen knew her now, she was sure.

After chores and breakfast, Dorrie helped Aunt Claire separate the milk. Then they weeded the garden before the sun was too high, crawling between the rows on their hands and knees. And they checked the strawberries, now whitish with pink-orange blushes on them.

"When will they be ripe?" asked Dorrie.

"Soon. A week. Two weeks. In time for the straw-berry social."

"Strawberry what?"

"Strawberry social," said Aunt Claire, sitting back and wrapping her arms around her knees. "All the ladies bake their best cakes and a pan of shortcake, and those with ice-cream freezers make up custard for ice cream, and everybody picks strawberries. And on a special Saturday afternoon we all go to the church and the men and boys crank the freezers, and the ladies slice the cakes and mash the berries and sprinkle sugar over them, and everybody brings a picnic tablecloth. And we eat and eat and eat." She grinned, and for a moment Dorrie thought she looked just like a young girl instead of someone old enough to be her aunt.

"Are we going?" asked Dorrie eagerly.

"Of course we are!" exclaimed Aunt Claire. "We'll wear our very best dresses, and I will talk with all the nice ladies and nod to all the handsome gentlemen, and you will run with the children and play ball, and maybe I'll even let you wade in the creek behind the church. And we'll have a hymn-sing and we won't come home until dark and the moon is out!"

"And is Adam going too?"

"Yes. Adam will go."

Dorrie thought a minute. "I can play with the girls in my Sunday school class, although I don't really know them all that well. And I can wear my navy blue dress."

Aunt Claire made a face. "Oh, dear," she said. "I forgot about clothes. You can't go in that dress."

For a minute, Dorrie thought she wasn't going at all.

"Oh, no," said Aunt Claire, seeing Dorrie's disap-pointed look. "I said you'd go. You just need a new dress, that's all."

Dorrie brightened.

"Let's see," said Aunt Claire. "I believe I've got some white cotton left over from the last quilt. Yes, and there's some eyelet lace on an old dress of mine in the upstairs closet.''

The excitement was back again.

Each evening after chores and supper, Dorrie sat watching while Aunt Claire worked at the treadle in the warm room, sewing yards of white cotton together. It didn't look like much of anything yet, but Dorrie knew someday it would be a whole dress. White, with lace trim. It would fit her. It would be her very own, not a hand-me-down from Cousin Myrna's Marilyn.

Sometimes Adam came over. Sometimes he told Dorrie stories about when he was a boy. Sometimes they would get Aunt Claire to stop sewing, and play the piano while they sang. Adam would sing ''His Eye is on the Sparrow,'' and Dorrie would get goose bumps. Sometimes the treadle machine would stop and Aunt Claire would say, ''Oh, shoot!'' Then Adam would wink at Dorrie and call, ''Everything all right, Claire-dear?'' It always seemed to make Aunt Claire mad to have Adam talk that way to her, and Dorrie wondered how he dared, but it was funny, just the same. And Aunt Claire never got so mad at the sewing machine or Adam that she didn't always give in and find something for them all to eat. Then, after Dorrie had gotten ready for bed, Aunt Claire would take up her Bible and read a chapter.

One night she read Psalm 27, and although Dorrie didn't understand all of it, some of the words were special and she savored them. *Salvation* and *temple* and *pavilion* and *tabernacle*. And the verse that said, ''When my father and mother forsake me, then the Lord will take me up,'' was a verse written just for her. *They didn't mean to forsake me,* she thought. *They couldn't help it.* But nonetheless, it had happened. And the words were comforting.

Then after Bible reading, Dorrie would climb the stairs to bed, and Aunt Claire and Adam would sit on the porch in the dark. The sound of their voices floated up the stairs, and Dorrie would fall asleep listening to the crickets and the frogs and the voices.

One rainy day, when there could be no gardening or playing outside, Dorrie opened the door of the room across the hall from her own and peered in cautiously. The wind whined and whistled around the corners of the house, and the summer rain drummed against the roof. Aunt Claire was at the treadle machine. The frequent whirring could be heard above the noise of the summer storm. "Go explore the spare room," Aunt Claire had said. "There must be some books in there for you to read."

Dorrie tiptoed across the threshold. Once inside, she could see that it wasn't one whole room, but two halves joined in the middle by an open archway. The first half was a small bedroom. The other half was an alcove, containing a secretary desk with a big glass-fronted bookcase, a chair, two trunks—a big one and a little humpbacked one—and several boxes. Dingy lace curtains hung at the windows, and everything was covered with layers of dust.

Dorrie walked on into the alcove. Through the glass of the bookcase she could make out the titles of some of the books. *Girl of the Limberlost*, by Gene Stratton Porter. *Eight Cousins*, by Louisa May Alcott. *Ruth Fielding and the Gypsies*, by Alice Emerson. *All these wonderful-sounding books*, thought Dorrie, *and no one reading them*. She opened the desk and discovered all the little pigeonholes and thought what fun it would be to fill them with stationery and stamps and postcards and secret notes.

Next she turned to the trunks. The little one looked as if perhaps it had once belonged to some other girl long ago. She opened the top. The inside was lined with faded lavender-flowered paper and filled with old photographs and albums.

There must be some pictures of my mother here, Dorrie thought excitedly, and she sat down on the floor and began lifting out stacks of photos. Most of them weren't the kind she had seen before, but were portraits mounted on stiff cardboard. Turning them over, Dorrie found each one had been named and dated. There were pictures of brides, of grandmas and grandpas on wedding anniversaries, school girls with plaid ribbons, babies in long white dresses. She found one of Great-aunt Eloise with another woman. Her grandmother? Great-aunt Eloise looked stiff and disapproving even then.

Then she opened an album, its cover yellowed with age, and found what she'd been looking for. "Margaret Manning, age ten" was written on the bottom of the portrait. Long black ringlets, bright eyes, a gleeful grin. Dorrie smiled. *I might look like that,* she thought, *if I had those clothes and had my hair that way.*

More portraits. Margaret and Claire as they grew. Claire younger, but with a solemn smile; Margaret mature, yet sparkling. And then Dorrie was looking at a snapshot taken on the front porch. There was mother, looking almost like mother, with a young-looking Aunt Claire; and behind them, leaning over the porch railing with grins on their faces, stood two young men. *Adam, and who's that?* wondered Dorrie. *Pastor!*

There were more snapshots of the four of them as Dorrie turned the pages. Pictures of them bicycling, picnicking, pictures of them with groups at the beach or at a Christmas party or in front of the church. Always those four together. Dorrie began to wonder.

Then she found the first picture of her father, standing tall and serious beside her mother. The next picture was of Adam by a shed, holding up a huge pig at least half as big as he was, and then of Adam in an army uniform. After that, she found no more pictures, only blank pages.

My goodness, thought Dorrie. My father must have come along and swept my mother right off her feet. And what about the others? What had happened to them between the time the pictures had been taken and now? And why were there no more pictures?

Dorrie closed the album and wondered about the four. She wished there had been some pictures of just two together. Then maybe she could tell if anyone had loved anyone else before her father had come. Maybe Adam had loved her mother, and had been left holding a pig! But she felt sure he cared about Aunt Claire, so maybe Pastor Linden had loved her mother instead. And what about Aunt Claire? She was always getting mad at Adam, so Dorrie doubted if she loved him. And whenever Pastor Linden was around, Aunt Claire acted almost too polite. Was that a sign of being in love? Dorrie sighed and shook her head. Love was a mysterious thing.

She carefully packed all the photographs back into the little trunk and closed the lid. Her mother was gone. There were still all those other people, Aunt Claire and Pastor Linden and Adam and her father. They were all rather alone now, though her father was being taken care of, and Pastor and Aunt Claire had the church people, which was rather like family. Adam didn't even have the church anymore, though Dorrie didn't know why.

And what about me? Dorrie thought. *Where do I belong?* She liked it in Angell better than anywhere else, but she couldn't see any reason why she'd be able to stay here any longer than any of the other places.

Suddenly she wanted to stay, desperately wanted to belong. But it was all so confusing, and she missed her mother and father so much it made her ache. She thought of the Bible verse about being forsaken, and she sat on the dusty floor, her face buried in her hands, and cried softly with the rain.

4
David
and the Plan

The lawn under the elms was littered with picnic baskets and checkered tablecloths by the time Dorrie and Aunt Claire arrived at the strawberry social. Adam had consented to go earlier to help the other men carry up tables from the church basement.

Dorrie drifted toward the church steps, as if the white lace she wore made her light enough to float. She leaned over the railing to watch a game of jacks.

"Want to play?" asked a girl named Trudy. Trudy had lipstick on.

"I haven't got a ball," replied Dorrie.

"That's all right," said a snuffly-nosed, kinky-haired girl whom Dorrie had never seen. She had a ponytail and a picture of a poodle sewn on the side of her full skirt. "You can borrow mine."

"This is Rhoda," said Trudy. "She's Miss

Crawford's niece from Elk Rapids. Have you been picked for baseball yet?''

''Baseball. Yuk,'' pronounced Rhoda, tossing her ponytail.

''I'm on Buddy Walters's team,'' Trudy went on. ''We're going to play after we eat. I hope Buddy picked Pastor's son too, because I want to be on the same team as Pastor's son.''

''Pastor's son?'' echoed Dorrie. ''But Pastor's not married.''

''He isn't now, but he used to be,'' snuffed Rhoda, confidentially.

Dorrie's mind went back to the pictures in the photo album. ''Excuse me, I've got to find Aunt Claire.''

She found her aunt with some other ladies in the basement kitchen, filling the cream pitchers.

''Oh, hello, Dorothy. Did you find someone to be with?''

''Yes—but there's something mysterious.'' Dorrie began to whisper and Aunt Claire, puzzled, bent her head down. ''Aunt Claire, does Pastor Linden have a son?''

''Really, Dorothy, this isn't the time to discuss—''

''Watch out, Claire, you're spilling the cream,'' interrupted a lady next to her.

''Oh, dear,'' cried Aunt Claire. ''Run along, Dorothy. I haven't time for questions.'' She turned away and began filling pitchers again.

Dorrie wandered away, dejected. She almost bumped into Adam at the head of the stairs.

''Hey, there, Dorrie,'' he said. ''Have you checked out that cake table yet? Better get there before—say, what's the matter?''

''Oh, nothing.''

Adam took her hand and led her to the shade of an old elm, where they sat down. ''Now, then, let's hear it,'' he coaxed her.

"I don't know what the matter is," protested Dorrie. "I asked her about what the girls said about Pastor's son, and she spilled the cream and made me go away."

"Hold on now," said Adam. "I'm kind of confused."

"Well, I was talking to the girls, and Rhoda, that's Miss Ida's niece—"

"You mean the kid with the poodle skirt and the stuffy nose?"

Dorrie nodded and gave a half giggle. "Yes, and she said that Pastor Linden used to be married, and had a son—and I don't believe them because I saw the photo album and I thought he loved either mother or Aunt Claire and besides, he *isn't* married. So I asked Aunt Claire—"

"Oh, boy," said Adam.

"And she spilled the cream and shooed me out."

Adam put his arm around Dorrie and snuggled her up beside him comfortably. She hadn't snuggled like that since before her father had gotten sick. Then Adam said, "Those pictures were all a long time ago, Dorrie. The girls were right. Matthew Linden has a son. He was married years ago, but his wife went away and took the baby with her. Nobody talks about it much."

"Why did she go? And what about Aunt Claire?"

"I don't know why she left. She was a city girl and I heard she couldn't stand being up here. Things weren't organized enough for her, and I guess she didn't fit in. As for your aunt, well . . ." He picked a long blade of grass and chewed the end, staring up through the treetops. "This is just between you and me," he said at last. "I think your Aunt Claire got some hurt feelings when she was younger. If you like somebody and they don't like you back the same way, well, that hurts."

"You mean Aunt Claire? And Pastor Linden?"

"Now don't you say a word to her, you hear?" cautioned Adam, sharply and quickly. "No woman likes to be reminded of lost dreams."

"Does she still—do they—?"

"Ah, now you're asking things I've no way of knowing—and no business knowing either, I guess."

"I saw all the pictures of you and Aunt Claire and mother and the pastor," said Dorrie. "I wondered where everyone fit. I wondered . . ."

Adam spit the blade of grass out. "Sometimes I think you wonder too much," he said a little gruffly. "Come on." He stood and pulled Dorrie to her feet. "Looks like the men are ready to make the ice cream."

The wind blew gently, and the afternoon sun filtered through the treetops, making dancing patterns on the tablecloths. And everyone ate until the men had to loosen their belts a notch, and the women were reluctant to stand up and clear away the dishes. So the grownups sat and talked, and some of the children began to choose up sides for the baseball game.

"Want to be on Buddy's side?" called Trudy.

But Dorrie shook her head. She didn't feel in the mood for a game anymore. Aunt Claire had said she could wade in the creek if she were careful not to get her dress wet. Adam pointed her to the little grove of poplars and willows behind the church.

It was curiously silent once Dorrie reached the shelter of the trees, and she was glad. It felt like stepping from one storybook picture to another across the page. Then she could hear the bubbling flow of water and the call of birds. A few more steps and there it was, an enchanting little creek that slid over golden sand and smooth, speckled stones under a leafy green canopy.

Downstream a big, sunny boulder lay in the middle of the water, and as Dorrie came closer she saw a round, brown lump on it. A turtle, sunning himself on a warm island. *Maybe I can sneak up and catch him,* she thought. It was hard to tiptoe through the water. Suddenly she heard a thrashing along the bank, and a boy

44

poked his shaggy yellow head out of the bushes.

"My gosh, do you have to be splashing around out there! You'll scare off all the fish!" He was a little older than Dorrie. They watched as the turtle launched himself into the water.

Dorrie turned on the boy. "You frightened my turtle, and now he's gone!" Actually it wasn't her turtle, but it might have been.

The two glared at one another, hands on hips.

"Hey!" called the boy. "Want to see the frog I caught? Bet you wouldn't dare hold him."

Dorrie waded back and climbed determinedly up the bank. She'd never held a frog, but she'd seen pictures of them in her father's biology books. They couldn't be all that bad to hold. She reached out her hands.

"Keep one hand cupped over him or he'll get away," admonished the boy, slightly wide-eyed.

Dorrie held him like he told her, and then with one finger she gently stroked his smooth, green head. "He's got such buggy eyes," she said.

"So he can see bugs," replied the boy, and they both laughed.

Dorrie looked up at the boy then. He had strange eyes, greenish, the color of the frog, with gold flecks in the centers. He needed a haircut.

"You can keep him for a pet if you want to. To make up for the turtle. Sorry I scared him," he said.

"Oh, that's all right," said Dorrie. "I'm sorry I scared your fish."

"I don't think there were any. They weren't biting, anyway." He picked up his fishing rod and wrapped the line around it, being careful to secure the dangling hook. "Are you at the strawberry social?"

"Yes," replied Dorrie. "I came with my Aunt Claire. I'm new here, I guess."

The boy grinned. "Me too. My name's David."

"Mine's Dorrie," said Dorrie, somewhat self-

45

consciously.

"Say, maybe it's time for seconds—let's go see."

"I have to get my shoes and socks."

"You can stuff the frog in your shoe and go barefoot, can't you?" David suggested, as they headed back.

It was just like Aunt Claire had said it would be. They stayed and stayed, eating some more, playing games, and singing hymns in the evening. The moon had risen by the time families gathered up their baskets and began calling good-byes to friends and neighbors.

"Are you coming to church with us in the morning?" Dorrie asked Adam as he helped fold the faded checkered tablecloth.

"No," he replied. "I'm going to spray the apples tomorrow."

"How come you like to eat here on Saturday, but won't come with us on Sunday?"

Adam gave Aunt Claire a quick look. "You put her up to this, Claire?"

"No. She's got a mind of her own. She can see."

Adam laughed and touched Dorrie's head. "Someday," he said. "Maybe someday." Then he strode off to his pickup and drove away.

When Dorrie and Aunt Claire got home, Dorrie set her shoes on the kitchen table.

"Off with your dress, Dorothy. That'll need a good washing," said Aunt Claire, reaching into the shoes for the dirty socks.

"Oh, be careful," cautioned Dorrie, suddenly remembering. "There's a frog in there."

"A frog?" exclaimed Aunt Claire.

Dorrie stuck her fingers down into the toe of each shoe. "Oh," she sighed. "Now he's gone."

"Well, I can't say I'm sorry," said Aunt Claire. "What was he doing in your shoe, may I ask?"

"It was a pet. From a boy I met."

"A pet? A frog?"

"Well, the turtle got away," Dorrie replied, smiling.

The next week brought Pastor Linden calling. And with him was a yellow-haired boy.

"David?" said Dorrie, bewildered, as they came up the porch steps.

His hair was combed, he had a neatly pressed shirt on, and he was no longer barefoot. "Hi, Dorrie," he said, with a grin. "How's your frog?"

"Hello, Dorothy," said the pastor. "I see you've met my son. Claire?" He smiled as Aunt Claire stepped onto the porch. "This is David."

Aunt Claire hesitated only a moment. "Well," she said, smiling politely. "So this is David. I wasn't aware Dorothy was acquainted with your son, Matthew."

"Oh, but Aunt Claire," said Dorrie. "I told you I'd met a boy at the strawberry social. I just didn't know he—"

"How nice," said Aunt Claire. "Please sit down."

"Well," said Pastor Linden, relaxing on the wicker sofa and stretching his arms along the back. "I thought, since David was going to spend the summer here, he should get to know some children."

"How nice," said Aunt Claire.

"Yes, isn't it," replied Matthew Linden, smiling at her. "And the first person I thought of was your Dorothy. As a matter of fact, I thought we might get together sometime, some evening. Take the children swimming at the bay, maybe make some ice cream."

"Well, I suppose that would be . . . nice," said Aunt Claire politely.

"Why, Claire, had I known how enthused you'd be about the idea, I'd have rushed over sooner!" Pastor Linden was chuckling now.

Then Aunt Claire began to laugh, and Dorrie was relieved that the strain had passed.

"Dorothy," said Aunt Claire, "why don't you two

run along? Perhaps David would enjoy the barn."

"Great!" said David. "I've never really had a chance to explore a barn. Mrs. Clark only has chicken coops."

"Come on, then," exclaimed Dorrie. "I'll show you the calf."

"Now that's what I had in mind," said Pastor Linden, approvingly. Then his voice was lost in the rush of wind that whistled past Dorrie's ears as she and David raced down the path.

Once inside the barn, she pointed out Bluebell's calf. "I can name her if I want to," she explained.

"What are you going to call her?" David leaned over the rail and scratched the calf's forehead.

"Nothing. Oh, it's not that I don't like Calfie. It's just that it's no fun to make pets you have to keep on leaving."

"What'd you call her?"

"Oh, Calfie? That's no name. That's just easier than saying 'Hey, you!' "

"That's a name," declared David. "Besides, this is your place, isn't it?"

"Not really. I mean, it is now, but . . . Where do you live? When you aren't up north, I mean?"

"I live with my mother and grandfather near Chicago. Grandfather's a preacher too. Would you like to hear a joke? My grandfather is a preacher teacher." David grinned. "I made that up."

"But what does it mean?" asked Dorrie.

"He teaches preachers. At a college. That's where my mother met my father. He came for dinner one night. Mother says she wishes she'd burned the roast. Then maybe he wouldn't have come back and they'd never have gotten married."

Dorrie was solemn. "I'm sorry about your folks. It must be kind of a mess—going back and forth. That's the part I hate. Never knowing when or where you're going next."

"But I don't do that," said David. "I always live with my mother and grandfather. This summer is the first time mother's ever allowed me to come up here."

"I'm glad she let you."

"Me, too. My dad told me about your folks. I guess you've got it lots worse than me. Is your father going to get better?"

"Oh, of course," said Dorrie. Then she grew wistful. "But I don't know when. It seems like forever, and I miss him."

"I miss mine, too. He comes to visit once or twice each year, but he and mother argue a lot."

Dorrie drew in her breath. "Preachers aren't supposed to fight."

"That's what grandfather said. But my dad said that preachers are human like everybody else. And we're all supposed to be good, anyway."

Dorrie didn't quite know what to say about that. "Do you want to play in the hay loft? There isn't much hay left, though. It's almost time to cut."

"Boy, I sure would like to help cut hay," said David. "My dad's told me a lot about it."

Dorrie looked at him. He was taller than she was. "How old are you?"

"Twelve," he replied, standing up straighter. "Going on thirteen. How old do I have to be?"

"I don't know." Dorrie shrugged her shoulders. "Maybe it depends on how badly they need help. We could ask Adam."

"Who's Adam?"

"Adam Campbell. Across the road. He does Aunt Claire's haying. Will your father let you?"

"I'm pretty sure he will," he said. "He talks about making a man of me, saying I need to grow up in the country. You know, fresh air and cow's milk and hard work."

"Well, I can show you the hay field," said Dorrie.

49

Together they ran through the barnyard, scattering hens and chicks.

At the edge of the hay field, David stopped short beside Dorrie. "Just look at it!" he exclaimed. "It's like the sea. Waves and waves, only they're gold. You sure can see a long way from here."

"You should see from the apple trees. You can see forever!" And they ran into the tumbledown orchard.

"You're lucky," said David, settling on the limb above Dorrie.

She peered up at him through the leaves. "I am?"

"Look at all you've got to play at." He made a broad sweep with his hand, knocking down a few green apples in the process. "A whole farm."

"I guess I never thought of it like that," said Dorrie.

"You like it here, don't you?"

"Oh, yes. It's just that you never know when you'll be sent on to somewhere else where they don't really want you anyway."

"Oh. I forgot. At least I always know I'm wanted. Isn't there any way you can make them keep you here?"

"I don't know."

"Well," said David. "Let's think about it, and maybe we can come up with a plan to make your aunt really want you to stay—and the others not want you at all. Then you can belong here. I'd sure want to stay here too, if I were you."

"Don't you like it where you stay?" Dorrie asked.

"Oh, it's all right. At least it's out in the country. But dad says if I can come up every summer, he'll start shopping for a place of our own. With me here, it gets kind of crowded at Mrs. Clark's."

"It's too bad you couldn't stay here," suggested Dorrie. "Your dad and Aunt Claire could sit and visit, and we could play together."

"I don't know," said David, with a frown. "That sounds like being married."

"Oh!" exclaimed Dorrie. "Why didn't I think of that?"

"Think of what?"

"Being married. Your dad and Aunt Claire. Wouldn't that be nice?"

"Well, I don't know," said David again. "That's pretty drastic."

"I know," agreed Dorrie. "But she can't marry Adam—all they do is fight. Besides, I think Aunt Claire wanted to marry your dad a long time ago, before he married your mother. Adam says. And if they got married, especially with your dad being the preacher, why, Great-aunt Eloise would *have* to think Aunt Claire was giving me a good home."

"Well, I don't know."

"Please, David, say you'll try it," pleaded Dorrie.

"Oh, all right," consented David. "Now what do we have to do?"

"Well, I think they should be together more. Maybe Aunt Claire should join the choir or Ladies Aid."

"And they should never argue. My mother and dad argued too much."

"Oh, David, wouldn't it be perfect?"

David just looked around from his apple tree perch and grinned.

Then they heard a truck laboring up the hill. "It's Adam!" Dorrie cried. "Come on, David, let's go ask about haying." They reached the driveway just as Adam was climbing out of the truck.

"Well, I see you've got company," Adam's loud voice boomed, as he headed for the porch. David and Dorrie joined him.

"Adam?" said Dorrie.

"Well, Claire," Adam continued, ignoring Dorrie, "I see the good pastor has come to call once again."

"Matthew just stopped by to introduce his son to us. Adam, this is David."

Adam turned and shook hands vigorously with David. "So glad you could come," he said, with a great show of enthusiasm. "I certainly hope you haven't eaten all that delicious cherry pie yet. Now, Claire-dear, you know there was some left last night."

Matthew Linden smiled. Aunt Claire turned red. "Adam, my heavens," she said with a nervous laugh. "Actually, I was just going to fix us each a bite."

"Not for us, thanks," said Pastor. "Tonight's choir practice and Mrs. Clark will have supper early. We don't want to keep her waiting."

"Oh, are you sure now—" began Aunt Claire.

"Now, Claire," said Adam, putting his hand on her shoulder, "you wouldn't want to interfere with Mrs. Clark's supper plans. You just get me that piece of pie now. Hauling a woman's chicken feed sure can work up your appetite, don't you think so, Matthew?"

"Well, actually—" began Matthew.

"Don't you help Widow Clark with her chickens?" asked Adam.

"Adam," interrupted Aunt Claire, "I'm sure Matthew—"

"Yes, I'll be going now. David?" Pastor and son left quickly, and Adam stood on the porch steps, one arm still around Aunt Claire's shoulder, and waved.

"Adam, let me go," protested Aunt Claire as the car drove away.

"Sorry," he said, releasing her. "Was I hurting you?" Dorrie didn't think he sounded sorry at all.

"Adam, that was the most ridiculous scene I've ever witnessed," said Aunt Claire, turning on him.

"How's that?" Adam asked with a faint smile.

"Why, everything you said was full of insinuations. About Matt being here again, about last night—"

"I didn't say anything about last night," said Adam.

"You implied that you'd been here till all hours!"

"Maybe I should move. Maybe the whole neighborhood thinks I come over here in the middle of the night to raid the refrigerator."

"Oh, Adam, don't be ridiculous. And then what you said about him helping Mrs. Clark. Adam, she's in her late forties and as ugly as a hedgehog! There's no way Matt would be courting her!"

"Why? Is he too busy courting you?"

"Adam! Get off this porch at once!" Aunt Claire shouted.

Instead, Adam collapsed wearily in the nearest wicker chair. "I'm not going to, Claire," he said quietly. "Last time he was here, I got so worked up I walked off and left my own truck here. I don't intend to do that again. Now just go get me a piece of pie."

"You act like you owned this place, Adam Campbell!"

He sat with his head back, his eyes closed. "Let me know when you want to go into partnership, Claire."

Aunt Claire went into the house, slamming the screen door behind her.

Dorrie had never seen Adam like this. First he'd ignored her, and then he'd carried on so with Pastor, and now he talked in such a rough way to Aunt Claire. He hadn't even said "please" when he'd asked for pie. It wasn't like him at all.

Suddenly Adam stood up. "Aw, what's the use," he sighed. He almost tripped over Dorrie on his way down the steps.

Aunt Claire came to the door with a piece of pie as he was backing out the drive. "Where is he going?" she asked. "Dorothy? Did he say anything?"

"He said, 'What's the use,' that's all," reported Dorrie. "What did he mean?"

But Aunt Claire didn't answer. She stood there a minute, watching him go and looking like she was about to cry. Then she turned abruptly and went back inside, leaving Dorrie alone on the porch.

5
Aunt Claire Betters Herself

It was haying time. Adam worked tirelessly all day, pulling the hay mower in dusty circles. Each noon he came up to the kitchen pump to wash, but he wouldn't eat the big dinners Aunt Claire and Dorrie cooked for the others, for Will Burton and David and ageless Mr. Waring.

Instead Adam sat under the apple trees with a cold lunch in a brown paper bag. He sat and ate, and Dorrie heard him singing songs. Not the joyful, confident songs she remembered him singing before, but deeper, darker songs. He sang, "Oh, Jesus is a rock in a weary land," and Dorrie, coming out to him one noon with a piece of berry pie, heard the words, "Shelter in a time of storm."

"Why do you sing that?" she asked. "There's no storm."

He gazed into the cloudless sky. "No, not up there.

But there are lots of kinds of storms. The song means that Jesus is a shelter in the storms of life."

Dorrie squatted down beside him. "Just like he's a shepherd, then." She watched a ladybug slowly ascend a blade of timothy grass. "Do you believe that, what you just sang?" she asked softly.

"I do," he replied.

"Then if you mean it, Adam, why—"

"Why don't I go to church?" Adam finished her sentence.

She looked up and nodded.

"This is church," he said, flinging his arms out to the trees. "As much as any building."

"But I mean the people. There are no people here."

"This is God's creation, Dorrie," he went on. "Isn't it beautiful?"

"But people are God's best creation."

Adam sighed. "Yes, I know. He made people for himself, to love him and talk with him. But most of them don't. They're just mirror worshippers."

"There, you've said it again."

"Look in a mirror and what do you see?" Adam asked.

"Myself," she replied.

"That's what people do. They worship their own reflections. They don't look at Jesus. They look only at themselves or at what other people think of them. They don't have enough love left over for God because they've spent it on themselves. They aren't sincere. They are hypocrites. I've seen it."

His voice trailed off, and then he went on talking, almost to himself. "I grew up in that church. It was all right for a while. The people I cared for were there. But your mother moved away, and Matthew went to Chicago, and Claire . . . I went off to the war, and when I came back, Claire had withdrawn into herself, it seemed. Then my folks died. Life wasn't as simple and nice as I'd thought it would be. And there just didn't seem to be any love left in the church, not for me. So pretty soon I stopped going."

"Oh, Adam," cried Dorrie, throwing her arms around him. "But I love you."

He put his arm around her and drew her close beside him. "There, now, I've said it. You kept wanting to know, and now I've told you. I'm sorry, Dorrie."

"But church people aren't all like that," she protested. "Besides, Aunt Claire says we're supposed to be like stained glass windows, and let God's love shine through us to other people."

"You're right. Matthew's a saint, manages to love us all. And your Aunt Claire, she tries so hard. But something in me can't be like them, and I can't go back. Can't, or won't," he added ruefully. He gave Dorrie his handkerchief for her nose. "I'll talk with God in the fields and you talk with him at church with the other people. But, Dorrie?"

"Yes?" She stuffed the handkerchief back in his pocket.

"Be sure you talk with him, wherever you are."

After David had worked all day, Matthew would come for him. Aunt Claire would often say, "Stay for supper, won't you?" And the four of them would drive to the bay for a swim and come home at dusk to sing around the piano. Aunt Claire would play "The Old Rugged Cross" and "In the Garden" and "Beautiful Dreamer."

"You should sing in the choir, Claire," said Matthew one evening.

"I used to," she replied.

"Yes, I guess both you girls sang," he recalled. "A voice like yours ought not to be hid under a bushel."

Dorrie and David laughed at the thought.

"Even David says you sing as well as any of the city

ladies in his grandfather's choir," Matthew went on.

The next Wednesday night, Aunt Claire put on a dress and began attending choir practice, and Dorrie went with her.

"You sing nice," said Dorrie, on the way home.

Aunt Claire, halfway through the first verse of Sunday's anthem, smiled.

"I don't know which you do best, sing or cook."

Aunt Claire raised her eyebrows but kept on singing.

"Everybody thinks Miss Ida is the best cook, but that's just because she always has ladies to her house for Ladies Aid. Nobody ever gets to eat your cooking."

Aunt Claire stopped singing.

"If you had Ladies Aid at our house, then they'd know," Dorrie went on, staring straight ahead. "Besides, Pastor always drops in, and I think that would be nice—because he'd bring David, I mean."

"Dorothy? Are you suggesting I have Ladies Aid at our house? I don't even go to their meetings."

"But don't you think you should?"

Aunt Claire gave a soft snort. "Dorothy, it's all I could ever do to get into a dress on Sundays for church. Now I find myself getting all fancied up if company's coming in the evening, and here I am joining the choir. And now Ladies Aid? You're quite a reformer."

Dorrie looked across quickly and saw the faint smile on Aunt Claire's lips. The inside smile—to herself, but it showed a little if you looked closely.

That Sunday, Aunt Claire invited the Ladies Aid to her home for their next meeting.

It was to be an afternoon luncheon meeting, and that morning Dorrie helped Aunt Claire get ready. While they were frosting little cakes, Adam stopped by unexpectedly with a bulb catalog.

"I don't need it, but I thought you might want to have a look."

Dorrie had noticed that Adam, having stayed away

all during haying, was now finding all sorts of little excuses to drop by lately.

"What are these funny little sandwiches with the crusts cut off?" Adam asked, stuffing one into his mouth.

"Adam! Don't eat those!" scolded Aunt Claire.

"Ugh!" he exclaimed after he'd swallowed. "What was that?"

"Cucumber and cream cheese," said Aunt Claire.

"Cucumber and cream cheese?" he echoed shrilly. "Cucumber sandwiches? Good heavens, Dorrie, who is your aunt trying to poison?"

Dorrie laughed. "They're for the Ladies Aid meeting. You'd better keep out of them."

"I will. I'll just try one of these instead." He popped a tiny cake into his mouth.

"Adam!" said Aunt Claire.

"Well, this tastes a lot better. But they must have shrunk when you baked them."

"They're called petits fours," spoke up Dorrie. "They're supposed to be small. Very delicate and dainty. For the ladies."

"Very delicate and dainty," mimicked Adam. "For Miss Ida. What's all this ladies' stuff anyway, Claire?" Adam helped himself to another little cake. "All this choir practice and Sunday school and Ladies Aid. And dresses, all the time dresses. What did you do with your blue jeans, burn them?"

"What's wrong with choir practice and dresses?"

"Nothing. It's just not you, that's all."

"Me! What do you mean, not me?"

"I mean, I always used to drive past and you'd be working in the garden or cleaning out the barn—your barn does need cleaning out, I noticed. And the garden looks like a shin tangle, and you're out mincing around with those silly ladies and singing with the pastor."

"I certainly don't think it's such a sin for me to be

trying to better myself a little," argued Aunt Claire.

"You were always good enough for me, the way you were."

"Besides," continued Aunt Claire, ignoring his last remark, "I think it might be good for Dorothy for me to be . . . more involved in things."

Adam turned to Dorrie. "Good for you? So that's it." Dorrie was suddenly uncomfortable under Adam's gaze.

"Well, I don't think I'll stick around here," he said at last. "I don't think I'm 'better' enough for you folks. Thanks for the petits-five." He took one more and headed out the door.

"Four!" shouted Aunt Claire.

"Three and a half," he replied from the porch, and then he was gone.

By two o'clock in the afternoon, all the ladies had arrived. Dorrie was a bit frightened at the results of her plotting. The peaceful, sleepy parlor had been transformed into a din.

Aunt Claire served her sandwiches, petits fours and coffee, while Dorrie passed the cream and sugar.

"Cucumber. How interesting," said old Mrs. Waring.

"Claire-dear, I do like your lovely flower arrangements," said Miss Ida. "However, might I suggest some cedar? Just a touch, mind you." Miss Ida smiled. "It makes a more creative bouquet."

"Are you out of eggs, Claire?" asked Mrs. Clark, timidly. "I only asked because we usually have deviled eggs."

"That's because I always ask you to bring them when we meet at my house," explained Miss Ida.

"Haven't you had your baby yet?" someone asked Halley Burton.

Halley smiled weakly. "Any day, the doctor says."

"Oh, my, I hope not today!" said the lady. "It

would spoil our meeting."

At last Miss Ida called the meeting to order, and Dorrie slipped out of the parlor and settled herself with a book on the front porch.

The ladies' voices floated through the screened door. "Do away with the yellow canisters and pass a special collection plate the first Sunday," and "The bandage-folding could be at your house," and another voice, Miss Ida's, with, "A touch of cedar always makes a more creative bouquet."

They're all talking at once, thought Dorrie to herself, amused. Then she lost herself in the book once more, in a gypsy camp with Ruth Fielding. But not for long.

From the parlor came the steady buzz of the voices, like bees swarming. "Deviled eggs or fried chicken?" Miss Ida was asking. And someone else was saying, "But not cucumber sandwiches, dear." And a third somebody tittered.

A car was turning into the drive. Pastor and David got out and joined Dorrie on the porch. "I see the meeting's well in progress," observed Pastor, nodding his head. He knocked at the door. "I'm afraid I'm late," he explained to Dorrie. No one answered his knock. He rapped louder.

"You might as well go on in. They'll never hear you," Dorrie observed.

The pastor hesitated, straightened his tie, and walked in.

"They're all talking at once," Dorrie told David. "Is it always like this?

David nodded and collapsed beside her on the sofa. "Every Ladies Aid meeting."

Inside the voices rose. Dorrie could hear the pastor say, "An opening prayer?"

And Miss Ida replied, "Of course. We can't have a closing prayer until we've had an opening prayer."

"Just hurry and pray, Matthew," urged Aunt Claire.

60

Presently the screen door swung open and out flocked the ladies, still in earnest conversation, gabbling like geese.

"I always pinch my fingers in those folding chairs." "And what's more, the celery is high in . . ." "Manure tea. Your roses will love it."

As the ladies descended the steps, Adam appeared and stood in the lily bed by the porch railing. "How's the meeting going?"

Dorrie laughed. "Oh, Adam! The meeting!"

Miss Ida was the last one out the door. "And I'll be sure and bring you some cedar clippings next time, Claire-dear." She waved and was gone.

Adam vaulted over the railing and onto the porch. "I see your dad's still inside," he said, nodding to David.

As if in confirmation, Aunt Claire's voice rang out above the noise in the yard. "I think it's perfectly ridiculous, Matthew Linden, to spend an hour discussing sugar cookies or molasses cookies."

"Now, Claire—" came Matthew's soothing voice.

"Or whether wooden chairs give your stockings runs or whether to use yellow canisters on third Sundays—"

"Really, Claire—"

"And I don't care if I sing like Florence Nightingale or not, I don't want to be in the choir, and as for—"

"All right, all right," said Matthew. "Nobody said—"

"Everybody said! Celery, not cucumbers, cedar in the daisies!"

"So much for that idea," said David.

"I guess it didn't work out so well." Dorrie looked dejected.

Matthew backed out the door and onto the porch.

"Well, Matthew," said Adam. "I hear Claire's got her dander up. I'm glad it's you leaving this time, not me."

Matthew gave a little sigh of relief. "Cedar in the

daisies?'' he echoed. ''I should have known this would happen.''

''And don't ever ask me to do another single organized thing! I'm not the socialite type!'' came Aunt Claire's voice. They could hear her rattling the teacups.

''Women,'' said Matthew. ''Lydia couldn't get things organized enough to please her. And Claire can't even survive a single Ladies Aid meeting. I'll never understand the creatures.''

''Well, all I can say is, it may not be me yet, but it sure looks like it won't be you.'' Adam grinned.

''What's that?''

''The winner.''

''Oh.'' Matthew blinked. ''I didn't know we were having a contest.''

''You know Claire,'' said Adam. ''She doesn't always play by the rules. Besides, I think these two know more about the game than we'll ever know.'' He nodded at David and Dorrie.

Matthew shook his head. ''Come along, son.''

Dorrie followed Adam inside.

''Claire?'' called Adam.

''I'm in the bedroom. I can't stand this dress any longer. What are you doing here again, anyway?''

''Well, if you want the truth, I'd walked down for the mail and on my way back I saw all the ladies leaving, so I thought—''

''I know,'' interrupted Aunt Claire, appearing in her faded blue jeans and shirt. ''You just wanted to say 'I told you so' and gloat in my defeat. Go ahead. Say it.'' She sat down on the sofa.

''Pretty rough?'' asked Adam, sitting down beside her. ''Did the ladies get to fighting?''

''No. Not really.'' Aunt Claire laced up her work boots.

''Oh, Adam,'' said Dorrie. ''It was wild.''

Adam grinned. ''Wild, eh? What's this about cedar

62

and cucumbers?''

"Oh, it's not their fault," said Aunt Claire. "They meant well. It's just not for me. I'm rather different, I guess." She looked at Adam. "I know. You already said that."

"Well, I'm just glad you found out in time," he said.

"In time for what?" Aunt Claire asked.

"Well, who knows how far you might have gone," said Adam. "One thing leads to another. First Sunday school, then choir practice. After the Ladies Aid meeting, you might have moved into the parsonage."

Dorrie gulped.

"Me? In the parsonage?" Aunt Claire laughed. "Adam, you're impossible." Then she turned to Dorrie. "Get changed and come on out in the garden. We've got work to do."

Adam sat staring at Dorrie after Aunt Claire had left. "Was I right?" he asked quietly.

"About what?" Dorrie said meekly.

"You know. First choir practice, then Ladies Aid, and next the parsonage."

Dorrie shook her head, concentrating on a crack in the linoleum. Her eyes stung. "Not quite," she answered in a small voice.

"Oh? What part didn't I get right?"

"The parsonage part."

"I see. Only because there isn't one built yet, right?"

Dorrie looked up. Adam's face swam into focus.

"Next time you go making plans you'd better make sure you check things out a little bit better first. Your aunt is a great farmer, but she might make the world's worst preacher's wife."

"I only wanted to—I just thought that if—"

"I know, it all sounded so grand to you. But don't forget about her happiness, too."

6
The Letter

The Harvest Supper was held at the church the Saturday before Labor Day. The next week would bring the start of school.

"I hope I get Mrs. Breckenridge this year," said Trudy. "Buddy Walters had her last year."

"Who's Mrs. Breckenridge?" asked Dorrie.

"A teacher, silly," replied Rhoda, who had come out with Miss Ida. "Mama says she's a true Southern lady."

"Southern? You mean Detroit, or—" began Dorrie.

"Oh, look, there's Halley Burton!" cried Trudy, pointing.

Dorrie turned and saw Halley sitting under the elms on an old quilt, nursing a bundle wrapped in blue.

"The baby!" exclaimed Dorrie. "Let's go see!"

"She's feeding him," said Rhoda, snuffing.

"So?"

"But she's nursing."

"Then we'll go ask Aunt Claire." The three girls found Aunt Claire talking with old Mrs. Waring. "Can we go see Halley's baby?" asked Dorrie.

"Why, of course," said Aunt Claire.

"But she's nursing. We just wondered . . ." said Rhoda.

Aunt Claire glanced across the lawn at Halley and smiled. "What do you suppose mothers did before bottles were invented? After all, Mary nursed Jesus."

Rhoda's eyes widened. "She did?"

Dorrie was delighted. "How else did he get his milk, do you think?" she asked Rhoda.

"I never thought of him eating," said Rhoda. "Except the Last Supper, of course."

"Well, it was the *Last* Supper, not the only supper," said Dorrie. "Come on, she's done nursing him now anyway."

The girls threaded through the tangle of children and grandmas to the spot where Halley Burton sat.

To Dorrie, it was like looking at a painting. The green of the leaves, the dark trunk against which the young woman leaned, the rich brown of her hair framing her rosy-cheeked face, the tenderness in her almost-violet eyes as she touched the baby on her lap. Dorrie wondered if her mother had looked at her like that.

Halley looked up as the girls approached. "You've come to look at my son, haven't you?" She smiled.

Dorrie squatted down beside Halley and gazed into the clear, dark eyes of the baby.

"What do you think?" asked Halley.

"He's so brand-new," whispered Trudy, awestruck.

"Can I touch him?" asked Dorrie.

"Here, put your finger in his hand," said Halley.

Dorrie felt the smoothness of his skin and then by contrast the strength of his grip. "My!" she whispered. "Isn't he strong? What's his name?"

"James William," replied Halley. "James for his grandpa and William after his daddy. But he's too little for all that, so we just call him Jamie Will."

"Jamie Will," said Dorrie softly.

The baby, suddenly sparked to life, began to kick his legs under the blue flannel blanket.

"Oh!" said Dorrie, startled, and the girls laughed.

"Cute little tyke, huh?" came a voice above Dorrie.

"Oh, hello, David. Have you already seen Halley's baby?"

"Dad and I visited Sunday." He knelt down on the other side of Halley. "Boy, he sure has grown."

"Come on, Trudy," said Rhoda, suddenly bored. "Let's go play jacks. Coming, Dorothy?"

"In a minute," said Dorrie. "He still wants my finger." Her eyes never left the baby.

"Oh, there's Buddy Walters—and he's got his new baseball glove!" Trudy jumped up and grabbed Rhoda's arm. Dorrie never noticed when they left.

In a few minutes, Will Burton joined his wife, and Dorrie and David, suddenly self-conscious, left them and wandered along the road in front of the church.

"I suppose you've got to go back home soon," said Dorrie.

"Dad's driving me back tomorrow after church. I've got to be home in time to start school Tuesday."

"School," muttered Dorrie.

"Don't you like school?"

"Oh, it's all right. It's making friends that's hard."

"I've been thinking about what we talked about in the apple tree that day," said David.

"Our plan didn't turn out very well, did it? Adam says Aunt Claire would have made an awful preacher's wife."

"I guess you'd better try something else. If there were some way you could show your aunt how much you really do belong . . ."

"I'm not sure what you mean."

"Well, like doing things to help her and letting her know how much you like what she does. Mrs. Clark thinks I'm a wonder, she says, just because I go out and help her gather eggs.''

"Oh, I see," said Dorrie. "But I already help a lot. I feed the chickens and I've learned to milk Bluebell and I wash the mason jars when Aunt Claire cans.''

"I don't know. Maybe you'll have to pray about it.''

Dorrie sighed. "I suppose I should have done that in the first place.''

Just then, Miss Ida Crawford emerged from the basement entrance, like a mole out of its tunnel, ringing the Sunday school bell. "Come along, folks!" she called. "Lots of real tasty food downstairs!''

After the blessing, while the dishes were being passed, Miss Ida turned to Aunt Claire with a smile. "I thought surely you'd be sitting next to the pastor tonight, Claire.''

Aunt Claire made no reply.

"Well," continued Miss Ida, "the way he's been calling on you this summer and you joining the choir and all, I just naturally thought . . .'' She paused a minute to help herself to the mashed potatoes and pass the bowl along. "I just naturally thought, well, you know what I mean. Can we expect wedding bells, Claire-dear?'' Miss Ida smiled, her fork poised in front of her mouth. Two peas rolled off it.

Dorrie waited breathlessly for her aunt's answer. It seemed as if everyone were waiting.

"Wedding bells?" Aunt Claire said at last. "Why, not unless you're getting married, Ida-dear.''

Across the table, Matthew Linden burst out laughing. "Miss Ida," he said, "you make the best coffee, and I'd appreciate it if you could pour me a cup.''

"Why, certainly, Pastor," said Miss Ida and, popping the forkful into her mouth, she struggled out from the two chairs she was wedged between and went off to get the coffeepot.

After supper, as Aunt Claire was packing up the picnic basket, David motioned Dorrie outside. It was that golden time on a late-summer evening. The sun was setting and the tops of the trees across the creek looked dipped in gilt.

"I know I'll see you tomorrow in Sunday school," said David, "but I thought I'd say good-bye tonight." He hesitated and studied the scuffed toes of his shoes then looked back up. "Good-bye."

"Good-bye," said Dorrie.

"Maybe next summer dad and I'll have a place of our own, and you can come over and visit."

"All right."

"And maybe Adam Campbell will let me help with haying again, and we'll work at your place."

"Maybe."

"Well, I'll see you next summer. All right?"

For a minute Dorrie didn't speak. She didn't trust her voice. It felt squeaky inside her throat. At last she said, "If I'm still here" in a half whisper.

David turned quickly and was gone.

The school bus let Dorrie out each afternoon at the foot of the hill, and she grew to enjoy the walk up the dirt road to the house. She would get the mail first, and then all the way up the hill she would look for birds gathering in the trees.

Only the red maples had begun to turn their fall hues. Their scarlet leaves stood out in contrast to the green of the sugar maple grove halfway up the hill. The fields were a sea of tickle grass, pale mauve, with islands of goldenrod here and there. The sky was most often a vivid blue, punctuated by brilliant white clouds.

It was that kind of day, the day the letter came. Dorrie was all the way up by the first rows of Adam's orchards before she looked through the small bundle of letters she carried. An electricity bill, a bill from the feed store, and a rather elegant envelope of pale blue with white edging on the flap. Suddenly Dorrie stopped. Somewhere, for some reason, she felt she'd seen it before. Then she read the return address with its flourishing letters, and she knew. She pelted the rest of the way up the hill and across the yard to the porch.

Aunt Claire was waiting at the door. "What's the matter?" she asked, seeing Dorrie's expression.

Dorrie came inside, handing her the letters. "That one, the blue one. It's from Great-aunt Eloise." Dorrie's breath was coming in great heaves.

Aunt Claire looked from the envelope back to Dorrie. "I suppose we might just as well read it right now. Maybe she wants to know how you're getting along at school." She opened it slowly, carefully, and read:

> My dear Claire,
>
> I am sure by now you have had ample opportunity to judge Dorothy Whitfield for yourself and to become accustomed to the responsibility of her welfare. However, I feel it my Christian duty to see for myself that all is well with her, and for that reason I will plan to be visiting you this coming Saturday. I had intended to come before school commenced in case other arrangements for the child were necessary. However, Myrna, who will be driving me up, has been indisposed until recently, so the trip had to be postponed until now.
>
> Trusting you are in good health, I remain Yr. Affectionate Aunt,
> Eloise Lang Carr

When she'd finished, Aunt Claire just stared at the open letter in her hands and then snorted. "Your affectionate aunt." Then she looked at Dorrie. "Oh, now, Dorothy, don't cry."

"I'm not crying," said Dorrie, wiping away a tear.

"Well, I hope not. It's only a letter. She'll just be here for a part of a day."

"But what if . . ."

"No what if," said Aunt Claire firmly. She quickly folded the letter back into its envelope and, opening the mica door of the stove, shoved the paper into the flames. "There now. Go change your clothes and play a while. There's lots of time before supper."

While Dorrie was upstairs, she heard the screen door bang and Adam's voice calling her aunt. She didn't bother to follow his explanations about the cattle sale until she heard him say, "Hey, Claire, this means money for you, and you aren't even listening."

Aunt Claire's voice replied, "Sorry, Adam. It's just that the letter finally came today. I thought that if we made it past school's starting, we were in the clear, but I ought to have known Aunt Eloise better."

Dorrie quickly buttoned her shirt, took off her shoes and tiptoed partway down the stairs to the crooked corner. The voices drifted up the dark stairs.

"Oh, you mean Aunt Eloisel, the Weasel?"

"It's no joke this time, Adam. She's coming."

"Coming? Here? What for?"

"To check on Dorothy. And on me, of course." Aunt Claire's voice was tight.

"Well, let her check," replied Adam. "What harm is there in that?"

"None. But that's not all. She spoke of 'other arrangements,' if necessary."

"But Dorrie's happy here," protested Adam. "There's no reason she can't stay. I don't understand what this is all about."

"Oh, Adam, don't be so naive," said Aunt Claire bitterly. "Let's face it—I don't live up to her standards. I never have. Nothing has since way back when my mother married my father and came up here. I'm sure this isn't Aunt Eloise's idea of a proper upbringing."

"So, spruce things up a bit. Put a tablecloth on the harvest table and give her lunch in here. Have your hair done in town. I'll even paint the house."

"I've gone that route before, Adam, remember? The choir, the Ladies Aid, the cucumber sandwiches?"

"Oh, come on, Claire," replied Adam angrily. "You know I like things just fine the way they are. But couldn't you make the effort for Dorrie's sake?"

There was no answer, and Dorrie held her breath.

At last Aunt Claire said, "No, Adam. I don't think I could. The Ladies Aid meeting was enough."

"Do you mean you want to have to give her up?" Dorrie had never heard Adam's voice so insistent.

"Since when does what I want matter?"

"Claire!"

"No. It wouldn't matter what I did—it never has. Aunt Eloise will do whatever she wants to, regardless."

"And you talk about faith," said Adam scornfully. "You're always at me about not going to church, but you don't even have faith to pray for what you really want, and for what's best for Dorrie, too. If you lose that girl through fear of trying, because of your own lack of faith, Claire, I'll—"

"You'll what? Never speak to me again?"

"Claire, I don't want her to have to go away. At least tell me you want her to stay."

"If I say I want her and lose her anyway, it would have been better to never have said it at all." Aunt Claire's voice trembled.

"No. You're wrong, Claire," said Adam quietly. "I wish I could make you see. But I never can, can I?"

There was no answer, and when Dorrie heard the door close and Adam's boots go quietly along the porch, she knew there wouldn't be any answer.

After Aunt Claire had gone back to the kitchen and Adam had been gone a few minutes, Dorrie crept down the stairs and fled silently out of the house and around the corner.

On the east side of the house, under the parlor windows, grew some lilac bushes. In front of the lilacs, whose lavender plumes had long since gone, was what Dorrie called the flower tangle. It couldn't be called a proper garden because no one took proper care of it. Now, at summer's end and fall's beginning, it was a mass of blooms among the weeds. Bright blue delphinium which had survived the summer storms; clumps of asters, maroon and gold; vermilion snapdragons, Adam's favorites; violet and magenta pansies, with the king on the throne when the petals were pulled away just right.

Dorrie crept in among them, her back against the lilac bushes, and looked out over the valley. Halfway down the hill toward the road was the grove of maples she passed each day on her way to the bus. At the foot of the hill was the old schoolhouse, now abandoned, where her mother had gone as a little girl. And at that corner, Aunt Claire's little side road met the main road which led to Angell Church and Williamsburg. Across the dirt road from where she sat were Adam's apple orchards, the red McIntosh apples already being picked. And across the open countryside she could see the farms of neighbors—Warings' red barn on the corner, Miss Crawford's yellow brick house down the road.

Her eyes began to blur. These weren't just names to her anymore. This was home as no place had been since her mother had died, and that place was little more than a faded memory now. She didn't want this place to fade, these people.

She hugged her knees to her chest and leaned her head down and cried. She cried for her mother and for her father, but mostly she cried for herself. Then she remembered. "When my mother and father forsake me, the Lord will take me up." And she whispered, "Please, Lord, take me up."

7
Great-aunt
Eloise

Dorrie sat at the bottom of the stairs, waiting, listening. She'd thought it all out, the whole desperate plan. While Aunt Claire had gone to Angell, Dorrie had lingered in the barn after chores, thinking, knowing she could never bear to leave the farm. Then, her mind made up, she'd hurried back to the house and stayed out of sight, in her room—until now.

"I hope you had a pleasant trip up," Aunt Claire was saying.

"Horrible," replied Great-aunt Eloise, "roads being what they are up in this part of the state."

"Yes, our car simply isn't used to such conditions," whined Cousin Myrna. Then Dorrie heard a new sound, a thin wail, and Cousin Myrna said, "Poor Baby-coo cried all the way."

"I rocked her, like you said," protested a plaintive voice. Cousin Myrna's Marilyn, who pulled off butterflies' wings.

"Dorothy?" There it was, at last. The summons she'd been anticipating, dreading for days now. "We have company to see you."

Dorrie didn't know whose face showed the most surprise as she stepped into the warm room—Great-aunt Eloise's or Aunt Claire's. The color drained from Aunt Claire's face. Great-aunt Eloise sucked in air with a ragged gasp, her upper lip curling back to reveal her crooked yellowed teeth.

Dorrie still had on her blue jeans and red plaid shirt, but now they were covered with dirt. Her barn boots were caked with muck, her black hair tangled with wisps of hay. Nonchalantly she put her hands on Great-aunt Eloise's bony blue-silk shoulders and stretched up to kiss the red-blotched cheek.

"Why, of all the impertinence!" exclaimed Great-aunt Eloise, brushing Dorrie's hands away. "Why, the child positively smells!"

"Stinks," corrected Marilyn. "Hello, Dorothy."

"Hello, Marilyn," replied Dorrie, looking at the familiar smirking face. Then turning to Marilyn's mother, "Hello, Cousin Myrna," she said.

Cousin Myrna, jiggling a sniveling baby on her hip, nodded and gave a brief smile.

"Claire," said Great-aunt Eloise, "what is the meaning of this!"

"Why, Great-aunt Eloise," said Dorrie, wide-eyed, before Aunt Claire could answer. "I've just been out working in the barn."

"Working? Claire, this is an outrage!"

"But, Great-aunt Eloise," continued Dorrie. "I worked for you when I lived at your house. Now I help out here—feed chickens, milk cows, shovel manure." She looked down at her muck-caked boots.

"Claire, is this true?"

Aunt Claire had regained her voice and some of her

composure. "She wanted to help with chores, Aunt Eloise. I must admit I didn't know about the—ah—manure, although it really does need shoveling."

"Well, I certainly never allowed her to work like that for me!"

"You didn't have any manure to shovel," explained Dorrie. "At your house, I cleaned the boarders' rooms, did up the supper dishes, helped with laundry, and—"

"Now, Dorothy," began Great-aunt Eloise, "every young lady should—"

"And how many boarders do you have now?" interrupted Aunt Claire. "I imagine you have a very prosperous establishment."

"Well, of course I have," replied Great-aunt Eloise proudly. "Presently I have five gentlemen and a lady schoolteacher."

"Quite a lot of dishes for a young girl, I'd say."

"Well, a little bit of work is good for the soul. Idle hands tempt the devil, I always say."

By now Cousin Myrna's baby had worked up to a full-fledged howl. "Marilyn, run out to the car for Baby-coo's bottle," said Cousin Myrna, jiggling the baby vigorously.

"Aw, ma," Marilyn groaned, making a face as she went out.

"Maybe we're all a little hungry," suggested Aunt Claire. "Why don't we go in the kitchen. You folks can sit down now while I put lunch on."

Marilyn returned with a triumphant look and a bottle which appeared to have been rolled in the driveway.

"Oh, Marilyn, the nipple!" wailed Cousin Myrna.

"I'll wash it off, Myrna," said Aunt Claire.

Dorrie sat at the table and watched the scrawny baby drink. "How come you don't nurse her?" she asked.

Cousin Myrna blushed. Great-aunt Eloise gasped.

"Ladies, modern ladies, that is, don't do that sort of thing anymore," explained Great-aunt Eloise. "It just isn't polite.''

Dorrie recalled Aunt Claire's comment at the Harvest Supper. She looked up quickly and caught her aunt's eyes on her and saw her head shake no, imperceptibly. Dorrie sighed.

"I'm not surprised that that's the kind of thing you're learning up here,'' Great-aunt Eloise went on.

"Well, it is a farm,'' said Aunt Claire. "And Dorothy does seem to enjoy helping with chores.''

"Chores. Milking,'' scoffed Great-aunt Eloise. "I suppose she drinks the milk too.''

"Certainly. She's been very healthy.''

"It won't last,'' predicted Great-aunt Eloise. "I certainly hope you have some pasteurized milk on hand. We simply can't take chances.''

"Yes, I went to the store especially for it this morning.'' Aunt Claire finished setting the food on the table, including two separate pitchers of milk.

"Which milk is which?'' asked Cousin Myrna, bouncing Baby-coo in one arm and straightening Marilyn's chair around with the other.

"Would you please ask the blessing, Dorothy?'' asked Aunt Claire.

"Dear Lord, for what we're about to receive, make us truly thankful. Amen.''

"Do you always do that?'' asked Marilyn, afterwards.

"Sure,'' replied Dorrie. "Me, or Aunt Claire—or Adam.''

"What for? Who's Adam?''

"Please pass the egg salad, Dorothy,'' said Aunt Claire.

"Which milk is which?'' asked Cousin Myrna.

"To thank God for the food, of course,'' answered Dorrie.

"Who's Adam?'' asked Great-aunt Eloise.

"Yuk, this egg salad has onions in it,'' said Marilyn.

"He lives across the road,'' replied Dorrie, her

mouth full.

"I asked who he was, not where he lived," said Great-aunt Eloise.

"I'm thirsty. I want some milk," said Marilyn.

"Which milk is which?"

"That one," said Dorrie. She neglected to point.

"Is it always this confusing?" asked Great-aunt Eloise.

"Not always. Sometimes," answered Aunt Claire, eyes on her plate.

"Especially if Adam's here," added Dorrie.

"Who is Adam!" thundered Great-aunt Eloise. Her face grew red.

"This one?" asked Cousin Myrna, picking up a pitcher.

"A neighbor boy," replied Aunt Claire.

"Yes, a big one," giggled Dorrie.

"Just pour it, ma," begged Marilyn.

After lunch, Great-aunt Eloise settled herself in the best chair in the warm room. "I see the parlor isn't open," she said, nodding toward the closed door. "Surely you must do some entertaining."

"No," answered Aunt Claire.

Great-aunt Eloise's eyebrows shot up. "No? No Christian service? No Ladies Aid?"

"I teach a Sunday school class."

"That's just for children," said Great-aunt Eloise, dismissing it with a flip of her hand. "I see you still haven't any indoor convenience either."

"What's a convenience?" asked Dorrie.

Marilyn snickered. "A toilet."

"Oh," said Dorrie. "I have a chamber pot under my bed. It has blue cornflowers on it. It's quite convenient."

"I never could understand," continued Great-aunt Eloise, "how your sainted mother, bless her soul, could survive up here. The day she ran off with your father, I said to her, 'Jessie Lang, you go off with that good-for-nothing Thomas Manning and that'll be the death of you.' And I was right, bless her soul.''

"My father was not a good-for-nothing," said Aunt Claire coldly.

"Humpf," said Great-aunt Eloise. "I say he worked her to death on this farm. And look at you: no better than she was. Worse. Working this place like a man—and dragging the child down with you."

"Mama," began Cousin Myrna.

"None of your sass, daughter. I came up here to do my Christian duty, and I won't be interrupted. I declare, things don't look a bit different than they did the last time I saw Jessie alive. It's a shame the child has to be raised in such circumstances. Now I tell you, Claire," she said, shaking a bony finger at her niece, "if I had the extra room, I'd take her away this instant."

Dorrie shivered, and Aunt Claire's back straightened as she stood there in front of the old woman's chair.

"In fact, I've half a mind to pack her things up this instant and leave her with Myrna."

"But mama," said Cousin Myrna, "All the beds—"

"Hush, daughter," said Great-aunt Eloise, lowering her voice and turning to Myrna. "A bed isn't necessary. All she had at my place was the sofa in the upper hall. Now," she continued, turning her hawk-eyed gaze on Dorrie, "stand up here, Dorothy Whitfield."

Dorrie obeyed, her knees weak.

"It seems to me you've been up here long enough."

Dorrie trembled. No one spoke. Even Baby-coo was quiet.

Then Aunt Claire broke the silence. "No," she said, stepping up to Dorrie, her arms encircling her from behind.

Dorrie turned to look up at her aunt's face. Her eyes

were ice blue and cold with anger, but her arms were warm and protective.

"No?" asked Great-aunt Eloise, rising slowly.

"No," repeated Aunt Claire, "she hasn't been up here long enough. It'll never be long enough. She was Margaret's, and now she's mine. She's none of yours. There's to be no more passing her around, no more of your judging us. It's all over."

Great-aunt Eloise's mouth fell open. "Why, this is an outrage!" she gasped. "I refuse to stay a moment longer under this roof!" She reached down for her purse. "Myrna! Get that baby wrapped up. Marilyn, get in the car!" She followed Myrna and Marilyn to the door and turned once more. "I've washed my hands of you, Claire Manning." She glared at Dorrie as she went out the door. Then as she stepped out onto the porch, she nearly collided with someone, and Dorrie heard Adam's voice.

"I beg your pardon, ma'am. Leaving so soon?"

"Oh! Well, I should say so, not that it's any of your business, whoever you might be."

Dorrie could see Adam now as he held the door for Great-aunt Eloise. He lifted his hat and nodded. "Adam Campbell, ma'am. And everything here is very much my business."

"Oh!" exclaimed Great-aunt Eloise, with a toss of her head. "This is outrageous!" And she stomped on down the porch steps.

As the car backed out of the drive, Adam stepped inside and stood looking at Aunt Claire and Dorrie. "Well?" he asked.

Then Dorrie left the circle of Aunt Claire's arms and leaped into Adam's, hugging him. "I'm staying!" she cried. "Aunt Claire told her off and I'm staying."

Adam held her against his chest. "You mean your Aunt Claire, that one over there? She told the old auntie off?"

"Yes, yes! It was wonderful—except when it was scary."

Adam's eyes met Claire's as he set Dorrie back down. "So you really did it after all, Claire," he said softly, with a look of wonder. "What did it finally take?"

Then Aunt Claire began to tremble, and she covered her face with her hands, and in one quick stride, Adam was beside her, his arms around her, and for the first time Dorrie saw Aunt Claire cry.

"Claire," he murmured softly against her hair.

"Oh, Adam, it was awful. I'm awful."

"No, not you," he said.

She sniffled against his shoulder. "Oh, yes, me. When I heard Dorothy tell how she worked for that old woman—Adam, she was treated like a hired girl! She cleaned and did dishes and laundry for the boarders and was made to sleep in the hallway. . . ."

"It's all over now, Claire," said Adam soothingly.

"But, Adam," protested Aunt Claire, "the worst part is that I wasn't loving her. I loved her inside me, but I wasn't loving her."

"I know," he replied. "You can start over."

That night Aunt Claire came upstairs after Dorrie was in bed. "Have you said your prayers yet?" she asked.

"Yes. I asked for daddy to get better. And I asked for forgiveness."

"Forgiveness?"

Dorrie nodded. "Because of today. I know now it was all wrong," she blurted out. "I had prayed about it, but then I went ahead all on my own. I thought I could make it better, and Adam had said to think of your happiness next time I got ideas. Honest, I didn't think you'd be unhappy if I looked and smelled like the barn. I just wanted to make Great-aunt Eloise not want me. I never thought she'd get angry at *you* for it and try

80

to take me away."

"Oh, Dorothy," sighed Aunt Claire. "I guess maybe we both learned a lesson. Isn't it wonderful how God works things out in spite of the tangles we make?" She bent to kiss Dorrie's cheek. "Good night," she said. Then as she turned off the light and stood in the darkness, Dorrie called her name.

"Aunt Claire?"

"Yes," she answered.

"I love you, Aunt Claire."

"I love you, too, Dorothy Whitfield."

It was November, almost Thanksgiving, when the second letter arrived. This time the address was "Mistress Dorothy Whitfield." Still, Dorrie didn't open it, but carried it up the hill with the rest of the mail. The trees were bare, and a sprinkling of snow lay on the empty fields, and it was too cold to stop and read. Besides, it was a bit frightening. Dorrie was at last beginning to feel at home. The letter was a threat. It could only be from someone down south.

She handed the bundle of mail to Aunt Claire, and then turned away, busying herself with boots and schoolbooks.

"Dorothy, a letter for you," said Aunt Claire.

"I know," replied Dorrie. "You go ahead and open it while I get my leggings off."

"But, Dorothy, it's your letter."

"Please, Aunt Claire," said Dorrie. "You won't let them change their minds, will you?"

"Change their—you mean Aunt Eloise? Oh, Dorothy!" Aunt Claire quickly hugged her. "I'm sure it's not from any of them. In fact, the handwriting looks a bit—well, you open it, dear."

Carefully, Dorrie opened the plain white envelope and pulled out the letter. She looked again at Aunt Claire, who nodded encouragingly, and then she unfolded it and read out loud:

My dear little Dorothy,

I did not want to write until I was sure. I will soon be released from the sanitarium and be on my way north to join you for Christmas.

I feel stronger each day, and look forward to the time when I can be with you again. I will be sending along some boxes which you may unpack for me if you wish. I'll send a telegram when I have consulted the train schedule. Be a good little girl. It is only a while longer.

Affectionately,
Your Father

By the time Dorrie finished the letter, her lips were trembling and tears were runnng down her cheeks. "Daddy," she whispered. "Oh, my daddy." And she buried her face in the sofa pillow and cried.

By the end of that week, the boxes began arriving. Every few days the phone would ring, and the man at the Traverse City depot would tell them of another box to be picked up at Angell.

The boxes began to pile up in the little pantry, and Dorrie was fascinated by the labels: Fragile. This End Up. Homestead, Fla.

"Oh," exclaimed Aunt Claire. "That's Florida. I believe that's where Oliver went one winter. Seashells, I imagine."

The crates continued to crowd the pantry. Do Not Freeze. Handle With Care. And a trunk with foreign stamps and strange writing, labeled Do Not Open.

"Where is this from?" asked Dorrie. "There aren't any letters in the writing. It's all just—just like tiny stick figures."

"Hmmm," said Aunt Claire, peering at the stick figures. "I would say Japanese. No wonder he says 'Do not open.' This box must be very special to Oliver."

Thanksgiving came, a somber, gray day, but inside, the house was warm and smelled of pumpkin and mince pies. It was after dinner—while Adam was having his second cup of coffee in the warm room, and Dorrie was lying on the rug in front of the stove feeling near the bursting point—that Aunt Claire made her announcement.

"Adam, I want you to dig me a septic tank." She said it very quietly, never taking her eyes off the little square of mica on the stove door, where she'd been watching the fire.

Adam slopped coffee down the front of his one white shirt, howled, and in reaching for his red bandana handkerchief in his hip pocket, spilled most of the remainder of the cupful on the slipcovered arm of the chair. "A septic tank?" he echoed, mopping himself.

"Yes, and while you're doing that, perhaps I really ought to recover those chairs," said Aunt Claire, eyeing the brown stain now well soaked into the padding.

"I'm sorry about the coffee. But, Claire, a septic tank? It's the end of November!"

"What's a septic tank, Adam?" asked Dorrie.

"Ask your aunt," he replied. "In November, no less," he continued, muttering. "Couldn't think of it in June or even September. Oh, no. Why not wait until February when the snow's six feet deep?"

Aunt Claire smiled her inside smile. "A septic tank, Dorothy," she said, ignoring Adam's mutterings, "is a lined hole in the ground where the pipes from a toilet empty."

"A huge hole in the ground," amended Adam.

"You mean an inside toilet?" said Dorrie.

Aunt Claire's smile widened. "Exactly," she said.

Dorrie had learned to trek uncomplainingly through the cold woodshed attached to the kitchen and across the short yard to the outhouse. But it was something she could never call a pleasant walk. Now, with winter coming on, she had been dreading those frigid mornings before school when she'd have to wade through newly fallen snow in below-zero weather. She thought of an inside toilet, white and new. "When?" she asked. "How soon?"

"As soon as Adam's finished his coffee," replied Aunt Claire.

Adam began choking on the last mouthful, which had escaped being lost earlier. Some of the coffee dribbled down his only tie as he sputtered. "Up my nose. Down my tie," he lamented.

"The tie is no great loss, Adam," said Aunt Claire, studying the orange circles on the purple background. "In fact, the coffee stains improve it."

"Why, I always thought it was rather nice," said Adam defensively. "Reminds me of the harvest moon." He winked at Dorrie.

Aunt Claire missed the wink. "It reminds me of big orange polka dots on purple. And I was only teasing about beginning today."

Adam began to relax visibly.

"There's only an hour or so of daylight left," Aunt Claire went on. "Tomorrow morning will be soon enough."

Adam groaned. "Are you really serious about this, Claire? For the love of heaven, the ground's frozen, and it'll take days and—"

"Now, Adam, I know the ground isn't frozen that hard or that deep. And I'm sure you must be just as anxious as I am to make Oliver's stay here as comfortable as possible."

"Oh, ho!" exclaimed Adam. "So now the truth comes out! You're trying to impress Oliver Whitfield—with a toilet!" Slapping his knee, he looked at Dorrie. "How do you like that? Most folks use nice manners and good food to impress company. But oh, no, your aunt's got to have a new toilet!'' And he roared with laughter.

But he was not laughing the next morning. Dorrie sat in the warm room, her chin in her hands, elbows propped on the window sill, and watched out the window while Adam began to dig what would become the biggest hole she had ever seen. He wore his sheepskin coat, a hand-knit stocking cap, and a heavy wool scarf around his neck and over his mouth and nose. When he breathed out, a fine fog appeared in front of his face. Every once in a while he'd take a break, lean on the handle of his shovel, and shake his head at Dorrie.

As badly as she wanted the new toilet, Dorrie felt sorry for him. So she kept a close eye on the clock, and every hour she would rap on the window pane, and Adam would nod and go around the corner of the house. Dorrie would skip to the kitchen where she kept a pot of coffee and a plate of cookies in the warming oven, and she'd meet Adam in the woodshed. It wasn't warm out there, but at least it was enclosed and out of the wind. Adam would pull the scarf away from his face, exposing his red nose, which he would blow fiercely. "Good coffee," he would say, gulping. "Your aunt's a heartless woman, Dorrie." Then, with a wink, he'd readjust the scarf and out he'd go again.

When school started after Thanksgiving vacation, Adam was digging before Dorrie left to catch the bus in the morning, and he was still there when she got home in the afternoon.

While Adam worked outside and Dorrie made popcorn chains, Aunt Claire worked on the new slipcovers. She had gone into Traverse City one Saturday morning, and returned loaded with all shapes and sizes of packages. Among them was a boxful of yards and yards of the most elegant fabric Dorrie had seen.

"Almost too good for chairs," Dorrie exclaimed. "Shouldn't we use it for dresses or something?"

"Too heavy," said Aunt Claire. "We'd look like sofas tipped on end."

Dorrie ran her hand over the material. It was a brocade, a delicate diamond-shaped pattern of small heathery roses and green leafy sprigs.

"Lovely," remarked Adam. "Will we be able to sit on them when you're through, or will we all stand around and just admire?"

But Aunt Claire was not to be deterred. "The green leaves match the rug," she said, "and I'll take the rose curtains out of the parlor and put them in here. It's too cold to sit in there anyway. And if I get out mother's good cranberry glasses for Christmas dinner, wouldn't that make a nice touch?" she asked Dorrie, who nodded even though she'd never seen cranberry glasses before, only cranberry sauce.

Adam shook his head and stomped off toward the woodshed.

As the days flew by, the kitchen was filled with the special fragrance that only Christmas brings—cinnamon and nutmeg, date filling for the *kolache* bread, whole cloves for making clove apples.

At last the day came when Aunt Claire stood in the pantry doorway, hands on her hips, and shook her head. "There's simply no room in this pantry for my baking and Oliver's boxes. Dorothy, run around to the septic tank, and ask Adam to stay for supper."

Adam came for supper, and that night in mid-December, he carried all the trunks and boxes up the narrow, winding stairs and into the alcove of the bedroom across the hall.

When Adam and Aunt Claire went back downstairs after the last box was brought up, Dorrie stayed in the bedroom. And then, with the wind swirling the snow around the corners of the house and whooshing in the chimney, she began to untie the cords and open the precious boxes that meant her father was coming.

8
Christmas and What It Brought

It was three days before Christmas when the telegram came, telling them of Oliver Whitfield's arrival time the next evening. Adam volunteered to meet the train at Angell while Aunt Claire and Dorrie finished chores and got cleaned up.

The house was all ready. The septic tank had been completed, and the new toilet hooked up beside the clawfoot tub. In the warm room, the new slipcovers were in place, the rose curtains from the parlor rehung. The Christmas tree stood by the window where earlier Dorrie had watched Adam dig the hole. She had gone to the woodlot across the back road with Adam to pick out the tree and help drag it home. Now its branches held a string of lights, all the colored glass balls from the attic, multicolored paper chains, ropes of popcorn and cranberries—and on top a yellow-haired angel with satiny-white dress and gold wings.

Beneath the heavily laden branches, packages had begun to pile up. Dorrie couldn't help it—she peeked and discovered that there were three with her name on the tags. She knew she had gotten gifts as a little girl at home, but that was too far back to really remember. All she could recall were a pair of gloves from Great-aunt Eloise last year, and before that, lace trimmed hankies from Great-aunt Mary. The thought of three presents, to be opened all at once, was almost more than she could take in. And surely her father would bring her a present too when he came.

On the night of her father's arrival, Dorrie helped Aunt Claire hurry through chores.

"I'll have Oliver here as soon as I can," Adam told Claire before he left, all bundled in his heavy sheepskin coat. Then he turned to Dorrie. "Have you in your daddy's arms before you know it."

Dorrie took her bath first and hurried upstairs to dress. Since Great-aunt Eloise's visit, there had been some additions to her wardrobe, and Dorrie still delighted in sliding the hangers back and forth on the rod. The dresser drawers, once so barren, were now full of pink panties and undershirts with rosebuds and all colors of socks and two new sweaters and a lacy slip. Quickly Dorrie tugged on one of the sweaters and slipped a plaid jumper over her head. Then she brushed her dark curls until they shone, and tied a red ribbon in her hair.

Downstairs again, she plugged the tree lights in and sat down to wait. And what was taking Aunt Claire so long? She picked up the bowl of Christmas cards and began leafing through them, looking for David's.

Just then Aunt Claire opened her bedroom door. Dorrie looked up, then stared in amazement.

"What are you staring at?" her aunt asked.

"Oh, Aunt Claire! You look beautiful."

"I guess you've never seen this dress before," said

Aunt Claire. "It seems there's never a reason to wear it. But tonight is special for you. A celebration."

Dorrie hadn't seen Aunt Claire in a dress, except for Sundays, since the Ladies Aid meeting. But this wasn't her plain Sunday dress. This was an aqua blue dress and it was soft, not starchy. What amazed Dorrie most was Aunt Claire's hair. She usually wore the tangle of red-auburn curls loose, or for Sundays, caught back by a ribbon. But tonight the curls were smooth and rich and swept up in a pile on top of her head, held by tortoise-shell combs.

Then, above the rush of the wind, the sound of Adam's pickup could be heard as it plowed through the drifts on the hill. Dorrie's heart skipped a beat, and Aunt Claire reached for her hand.

"Now remember, your father's just out of the hospital," she said. "He's likely to be tired and, well, maybe not quite like he was."

"Oh, it doesn't matter," replied Dorrie. "Only that he's here."

Suddenly there were footsteps on the porch, and the door flew open, and out of the dark and snow and into the Christmas-tree-and-lamplight glow of the warm room stepped a tall, slender man. The weight of his greatcoat seemed almost too heavy for his shoulders to bear. His sandy hair was flecked with snow, and his brown eyes were tired, but there was the beginning of a smile on his pale face.

"Dorothy? Dorothy Margaret?"

"Daddy!" cried Dorrie, and flew into his outstretched arms.

Aunt Claire had tea and hot chocolate ready on the back of the stove, and as soon as the men had shaken off the snow and shed their heavy coats and scarves and boots, she led them into the kitchen. Dorrie clung to her father's arm.

"Oh, Oliver, it's so wonderful to see you again,"

said Aunt Claire, not for the first time. "More tea? You must be freezing."

"Thank you, yes. I must admit, if Adam hadn't been right there, I might be a solid block of ice by now." Oliver nodded gratefully to Adam, whose eyes had hardly left Aunt Claire's face.

"I'm so glad you got here in time for Christmas," Aunt Claire went on. "You'll be able to hear Dorothy speak her piece tomorrow night at church."

"It's been a long time since I've been to church on Christmas Eve," said Oliver wistfully, his brown eyes far away. "In fact, it's been a long time since I've really celebrated Christmas at all."

"Oh, daddy, was it awful for you?" Dorrie took his hand and pressed it against her cheek.

Oliver sighed and smiled at her.

"Plenty of time to talk tomorrow," said Aunt Claire. "It's way past your bedtime, Dorothy."

"Mine, too," said Adam, rising from the table. "Oliver, it's good to have you here." Oliver stood and the two men shook hands.

"Thank you again, Adam."

"Good night, Dorrie." Adam bent down to give her a kiss.

"Good night, Adam."

"Claire?" He stood facing her, his eyes taking in the blue of her dress, the blue of her eyes. "I wish it were all for me."

"But . . . it's a special day for Dorothy," Aunt Claire said awkwardly.

"I see," he replied at length. "Well, good night." And picking up his sheepskin coat, he left quickly.

"He forgot his boots," exclaimed Oliver. "He's out there in all that snow without his boots on."

"He's that way sometimes," sighed Aunt Claire.

"Yes," said Dorrie. "Once he forgot his truck and walked home."

"Bedtime, Dorothy," said Aunt Claire.

The next morning, Christmas Eve day, Dorrie helped her father unpack. The bedroom and alcove across the hall were now overflowing with boxes and being transformed into an exotic world. Dorrie was spellbound. The books from the oak secretary had been put in Dorrie's room and replaced by Oliver's biology books and shell collections. Shallow boxes and trays of rock samples lined the walls. One table held huge bottles of preserved eels and strange fishes, while a second table was stacked with more books and reams of writing paper. Pictures of green frogs and delicate underwater creatures now hung where the Manning ancestors had been.

"What are they?" asked Dorrie, pointing to the pictures.

"Jellyfish, Portuguese man-of-war, sea anemone, starfish."

"And what was in the special box? Aunt Claire said it might have come from Japan."

Dorrie's father looked pleased. "It is a Japanese box," he said. "Come see." And opening the box, he lifted out tray after tray of shells, delicate pastel colors.

"Oh, they're beautiful," whispered Dorrie.

"And very special too," added her father. "They are found only in Japan. Nowhere else in the world. I traded some of my mollusks for these just before the war. You don't remember these things at all, do you?"

"No."

Oliver sighed. "You were quite young. I'm sorry it's been so hard for you. I couldn't help it."

"It's all right now, daddy."

"I kept trying to make things better. I kept trying to make everything change. But it wouldn't." He sat down. Dorrie came up and put her hand on his shoulder. "I wanted it all to be different for us. But it kept getting worse, and I couldn't stop it. And instead of more of us, there kept getting less of us."

"Less of us?"

"There was a baby, Dorothy. A baby brother for you. But he died. And then Margaret, your mother, died. And they took you away, and I thought for a long time I'd go next."

Dorrie laid her wet cheek against his sandy hair. "But we're fine now, aren't we?"

"Oh, yes." He pulled a handkerchief out of his pocket and blew his nose vigorously. Then he drew Dorrie down on his lap. "Yes, we're just fine now."

"I'm sure it's because of God and the prayers," said Dorrie, smoothing down his collar. "Aunt Claire's taught me to say prayers again. I'd forgotten at Great-aunt Eloise's."

He sighed. "I knew it would be all right as soon as I heard you were coming here. It's good for you here, isn't it?" he asked.

Dorrie grinned. "Oh, yes, daddy. You'll see. And it'll go on and on forever, won't it?" She snuggled against him.,

"Dorothy?"

"Hmmm?"

"It might—no, never mind."

That evening at the Christmas program, Dorrie thought she was the happiest she'd ever been. She stood at the front of the church and looked out at the crowd of familiar faces, seeking those that belonged to her. Adam, looking self-conscious in his brown tweed Sunday suit, sat on one side of Aunt Claire. Her red curls were done up neatly, and she was wearing the aqua blue dress. "The color of the Mexican Gulf," Oliver had complimented her before they'd left the house. "The color of her eyes," Adam had countered. On the other side of Aunt Claire sat Dorrie's father.

The next thing she knew, Pastor was nudging her gently and it was her turn. Proudly she stepped forward and began, "And the angel said unto them, Fear not: for, behold, I bring you good tidings of great joy. . . ."

After Christmas Oliver spent most of each day in his room, leafing through volumes of books or hunched over his desk, writing.

And Dorrie did some writing of her own: a letter to David. Sitting cross-legged in the middle of her bed, she quickly came to the heart of her letter:

> I don't have to go back to Great-aunt Eloise or anyone. But I worry about daddy. Do you suppose it would be all right if we prayed for him to marry Aunt Claire? Then we would all be a family.

When she'd finished, she reread the letter, hoping it sounded all right. It was a rather selfish prayer, but at least it was a prayer, and wasn't it for the best? Didn't her father need looking after, and shouldn't Aunt Claire have a husband?

She heard footsteps on the stairs and then a knock on her father's door. "Oliver?" said Aunt Claire. "I've brought you a pot of tea and some fresh bread."

"Come in," replied Dorrie's father. "I'm afraid you are babying me too much, Claire."

Aunt Claire laughed softly. "Nonsense, Oliver. You need someone to fuss over you a bit. Besides, we're so happy just to have you here and healthy, we can't help ourselves. How is the book coming?"

"Slowly. I guess that's the only way to write a book."

"I think it's marvelous, Oliver. I'm sure I won't understand a thing you've written, but I think it's marvelous, just the same."

"Thank you, Claire," said Oliver.

When her aunt came into the hall again, Dorrie called to her, stuffing the letter quickly under her pillow.

Aunt Claire came in and sat on the edge of the bed, giving Dorrie a hug.

"It's nice having daddy here, isn't it?" said Dorrie.

"Oh, Dorothy, you know how worried we've been about him."

"And you do like him, don't you?"

"Oh course," said Aunt Claire. "You know how fond of him I am."

Dorrie's heart beat a little faster. "I suppose you're fonder of him than of Pastor Linden."

"Well, after all, he is your father."

"Fonder than Adam?" asked Dorrie. She shut her eyes tight, waiting.

"Why, Dorothy, what's this all about?"

"Oh, I just wanted to know if having daddy here makes you happy."

"Why, you know it does. I think it's wonderful."

Dorrie was delighted. By her own admission, Aunt Claire was happy with her father. She grinned and snuggled back down against Aunt Claire. "I hope it'll be like this forever," said Dorrie.

Aunt Claire kissed Dorrie's forehead and stood up. "I hope you're always this happy, that's what I hope." And she went downstairs.

I know one thing, thought Dorrie. *If daddy married Aunt Claire, I would be this happy always. And it would be like this forever.*

The next day Adam came calling for Dorrie. It was the last day of Christmas vacation, and he'd promised to take her tobogganing before school started again. He sat in the kitchen, sipping coffee, while Dorrie pulled on her leggings and bundled up.

"Well, have you had a good vacation?" Adam asked.

"Yes, wonderful!" she exclaimed.

"I haven't seen you much," he said. "Too busy to come visit me?"

"I have been sort of busy, with daddy here and all." She struggled with her boots. "How come you haven't visited us?"

Adam raised an eyebrow at Aunt Claire, who was watching from the kitchen doorway. "Oh, I don't know. Busy, I guess. Been gone a lot too. Celebrating the holidays, you know."

"Gone? But, Adam, you were home New Year's Eve. I looked across and could see your lights on all evening."

"Hmm," he said, "Must have left a light on when I went out."

Dorrie stood up. "No. You always leave your kitchen light on. But your living room lamp was on too. And I saw the bedroom light go on and off."

"You're getting to be a regular neighborhood snoop," he teased, pulling her stocking cap down over her eyes. "You ought to hire out to Miss Ida. Now get a move on, I'm sweltering."

"Going sledding, I see," said Oliver, coming into the kitchen. "Nice of you to take her out like this, Adam."

"I enjoy it," replied Adam. "Why don't you come too, Claire?"

"Heavens, no," replied Aunt Claire. "Why would I want to do a thing like that?"

"You always used to like it. Remember?" Then to Oliver, he explained, "We've all gone tobogganing since we were kids."

"When we were kids," corrected Aunt Claire.

"You went with me last year," said Adam. "Or have you forgotten?"

"Well, I'm not going now."

"Daddy, why don't you come?" suggested Dorrie.

"Oh, Dorothy, I think I'd better not."

"Your father might not feel quite up to it," said Adam.

"It isn't that so much as—" began Oliver.

"He has an awful lot of work to do too," put in Aunt Claire.

"Well, it's not—"

"You've never taken me tobogganing before," said Dorrie, in a quiet voice.

"Actually," said Oliver, "I am feeling quite fit, and I've just begun a new chapter so it'll be easier to pick up where I left off. I just didn't want to interfere with Adam's plans."

Dorrie grasped her father's hand. "Oh, please come then. We want you to." She turned to Adam for support.

"Sure, Oliver," said Adam, politely. "Be glad to have you."

The air was crisp and clear, and they were partially protected from the northwest wind as they tobogganed down the hill's eastern slope. The late morning sun warmed them.

"Perfect day for it," said Adam, pulling the toboggan as they climbed upward for another run.

"I haven't felt this good in a long time," said Oliver. "It must be this fresh country air."

"It makes a man of you," said Dorrie.

"What's that?" asked her father.

"That's what David's father told him."

"Matthew Linden," explained Adam. "His boy, David, was up from Chicago this past summer."

"Oh," said Oliver. "I didn't know he'd married. From Chicago?"

"Left here right after you and Margaret did. Married the daughter of one of his professors down there, but it didn't work out."

"That's too bad."

"Happens sometimes, I guess," said Adam. "David's a bit older than Dorrie. Nice boy."

"I always thought maybe Matthew and Claire . . ." began Oliver.

"I guess she thought so too for a while."

"Thought what?" asked Dorrie.

96

They had reached the crest of the hill.

"What happened?" Oliver inquired.

Adam shrugged his shoulders. "Matt just went off to school, and when he came back, he brought Lydia. That was the end of that."

"Oh, you mean David's mother?" asked Dorrie.

"Why don't you two go down together this time," suggested Adam.

"I know," said Dorrie. "You're talking about when Aunt Claire was in love with the pastor, back in the old days when the pictures were taken. But she doesn't love him anymore."

"Why, Dorothy!" exclaimed her father with a surprised grin. "How do you know about those sorts of things?"

"I saw the pictures upstairs in a trunk. Aunt Claire liked him, but I guess he didn't like her back. Isn't that right, Adam?"

"She's amazing," said Adam, half under his breath, staring up at the sky. "Get on the toboggan, Dorrie."

"Well, I'm glad they never got married anyway," continued Dorrie.

"Fine. Me too," said Adam impatiently. "Now will you get on?" He lifted her onto the toboggan. "You're next, Oliver," he said.

Oliver sat down behind Dorrie, wrapping his arms around her.

"Ready?" called Adam, beginning to push the toboggan.

"I'm glad," shouted Dorrie, "because now she can marry daddy!"

The toboggan shot off down the hill.

When Oliver and Dorrie arrived back at the top again, Adam was swinging his arms about and jumping. "Cold," he explained. "You can keep on sliding, but I think I'll go on home."

"Oh, no thanks," said Oliver. "I've stayed out long

enough. That last climb rather did me in, I'm afraid. Come on, Dorothy.''

"Well, suit yourself," said Adam, as they all headed back toward the house. "I won't be needing the toboggan anyway. Why don't you keep it up at Claire's?''

"Oh, could we? Then I could go sliding anytime!" Dorrie clapped her mittened hands.

"Awfully nice of you, Adam," said Oliver. "By the way, I think I should explain. Dorrie ought not to have said what she did back there.''

"What's that? Oh, about you and Claire?" Adam gave a short laugh. "I guess Dorrie can say whatever she wants to.''

"Well, it's just that—" began Oliver.

"What I was saying was—" interrupted Dorrie.

"Look, you don't need to feel you owe me any explanation," said Adam, as they reached the back porch. "If you and Claire—"

"That's what I want to explain," insisted Oliver.

"Yes, daddy and Aunt Claire—" piped up Dorrie.

The kitchen door had opened. "Daddy and Aunt Claire what?" asked Aunt Claire. "And for heaven's sake, come in where it's warm and have some hot chocolate.''

"Not for me, thanks, Claire. I've got to be going," said Adam.

"What I was saying was—" began Dorrie, eager to have it said.

"Dorothy, not now," said her father firmly.

Dorrie's smile faded.

"Be seeing you, Claire," said Adam, and he stepped backward off the porch, lurching awkwardly in the deep snow.

"Adam?" said Aunt Claire in alarm.

But he righted himself, gave a short wave, and stalked off across the yard toward his own house.

9
Not Happily
Ever After

Dorrie was in heaven. It looked as if her plans would finally turn out right. Of course, nobody had said anything, but maybe love was different when you were older and had been married once, as her father had. Besides, nobody had said they *weren't* getting married. She began watching Aunt Claire closely for signs.

"Oliver, be sure to wear your boots and take an extra scarf if you're going down for the mail," cautioned Aunt Claire one Saturday afternoon in late January.

"I think I can remember to put boots on, thank you," he replied, with a wink to Dorrie. "You must think I'm a child, Claire."

"Oh, Oliver, I'm sorry, I didn't mean—" Aunt Claire stopped pumping the treadle and turned quickly from her sewing.

Oliver was struggling into his greatcoat. "Oh, I was just teasing, Claire. I know you're concerned. I wish you wouldn't be."

"Well, it's just—I can't seem to help it," said Aunt Claire. "What would I do if you got sick or something?"

Oliver wrapped the extra scarf around his face. "At least then you'd have a better reason to fuss over me than you do now."

After he'd left, Dorrie scooted the footstool over by the sewing machine to watch Aunt Claire work on the new blue dress.

"When's it going to be done?" she asked.

"Maybe in time for church tomorrow. We'll both have a blue dress to wear, then." Aunt Claire snapped off the threads at the end of a seam and held it up for Dorrie. "Well, what do you think?"

"Looks kind of funny with only one sleeve," replied Dorrie.

"Wait until it's finished, then," said Aunt Claire, laughing. "I thought maybe your daddy would like the color." She held it away from her and gave it a critical stare, then smiled.

Faraway, thought Dorrie, watching her. *She looks faraway—that must be a sign.* She wasn't sure, of course, but by the next day, the sign was confirmed by someone who should know.

"Why, Dorothy Whitfield, I do declare, a new dress!" exclaimed Miss Ida Crawford, bustling up to them after the benediction. "Why, the child looks like a breath of spring, and in the middle of the winter," Miss Ida continued. "Thanks to you, Claire-dear."

"Thank you, Ida," replied Aunt Claire.

"Both of you girls in blue," Miss Ida went on. "Don't you think Claire chooses such lovely colors, Mr. Whitfield?"

Oliver smiled slowly. "I do indeed, Miss Crawfold. Both of them look very nice in blue."

"Matches your eyes, Claire-dear," said Miss Ida,

"which, by the way, have a definitely dreamy look."

"Oh, for goodness' sake!" protested Aunt Claire, turning red.

"Definitely dreamy," repeated Miss Ida.

"Come along, Dorothy," said Aunt Claire. "Nice to see you, Ida."

Oliver offered his arm to Aunt Claire as they approached the icy steps where Pastor Linden stood greeting his flock.

"Lovely family." They could hear Miss Ida's voice behind them, floating above the other voices. "Don't you think so, Mrs. Waring?"

"Glad to see you looking so well, Oliver," said Pastor Linden.

"Matthew," said Oliver. The two shook hands.

"We haven't seen you in a long time," said Aunt Claire. "Why don't you come over some evening?"

"I've been meaning to. But there always seems to be something. If it isn't Missionary Society, it's a board meeting—"

"Or we're snowed in," interjected Oliver.

"Well, do come," said Aunt Claire. "Any evening is fine."

A special invitation to the pastor—Dorrie was convinced now that there must be special plans to be discussed.

She was overjoyed when, a week later, Matthew did come.

"Heard there was a storm headed our way," he explained as Aunt Claire took his coat and hat. "I was afraid if I didn't get up here now, I might not make it until Easter!"

Oliver smiled. "I sometimes think I won't see the outside world until spring. I must admit, I do miss green."

"Green?" echoed Aunt Claire, as they settled in the warm room.

"I mean growing things, Claire," Oliver explained.

"I hear from Dorothy that you're writing a book," said Matthew.

"From Dorothy?" Oliver glanced at his daughter, surprised.

Matthew grinned. "Somehow she manages to keep me well-informed."

"Adam was right—she is amazing," said Oliver.

"Speaking of Adam," said Matthew, "I hear he's been sick. Miss Ida Crawford saw him in at the doctor's office the other day."

"Oh," said Aunt Claire. "I hadn't heard."

"Bad cold, I guess. I'm stopping in on him before I go home."

"Well, be sure to give him our best," said Oliver.

Aunt Claire passed around the coffee cups, and Dorrie nestled by the stove, listening attentively to the talk, waiting.

"Isn't it about bedtime, Dorothy?" asked Aunt Claire at last.

"Oh," said Dorrie anxiously, "but I don't want to miss anything."

Pastor laughed. "And what do you think you might miss?"

Dorrie glanced from her father to Aunt Claire. "Oh, I don't know. Plans, maybe."

"Speaking of plans, I do have some news for you," said Pastor.

Dorrie held her breath.

"I've been talking to Halley and Will Burton. Seems Halley's mother is getting too old to live on the old place alone, and they're thinking of moving out of the cottage and into the big farmhouse."

"Oh, I'm sorry to hear that," said Aunt Claire.

"Yes," agreed Pastor. "But I was thinking about the cottage. I thought if I could buy it or at least rent it, then David could spend summers up here in our own place."

"Oh, Pastor!" Dorrie beamed. "That would be perfect!"

"That is good news, Matthew," said Aunt Claire.

"I'd sure appreciate your prayers," said Matthew. "It's nice to have a place you can settle down in and call home, eh, Oliver?"

"What? Oh. Yes, I suppose so," said Oliver, absent-mindedly.

"Well," said Matthew, at last. "I guess it's time to go. Have to drop in on Adam yet."

Dorrie was disappointed. How could he go? The marriage plans hadn't been discussed yet. "I'm going to bed now," she announced suddenly, "just in case you want to kind of talk privately." Maybe they just needed a little encouragement. She kissed her aunt and her father good night and climbed the dark, cold stairs. As she was falling asleep, thoughts of weddings drifted through her mind. Lace and roses and satin ribbons.

The next morning, as soon as she woke up, Dorrie hurried into her father's room. He was already dressed and working at his desk.

"Good morning, daddy," said Dorrie, climbing into his unmade bed and warming her feet under the covers. "Did you have a nice visit with Pastor last night?"

"Yes. But you know that. You were there."

"But what about after I went to bed?" asked Dorrie, hopefully.

"After you went to bed, Pastor went home."

"Didn't you talk about any special plans or anything?"

"Look here, Dorothy," said her father. "Just what is it you're getting at? I mean, what's all this about special plans?"

Dorrie gazed into her father's serious brown eyes and gulped. "Well, I just thought—I mean, aren't you and Aunt Claire—well, it's just so perfect, daddy, and—"

"Dorothy, aren't Aunt Claire and I what?"

"Getting married?" said Dorrie in a tiny voice, hugging her knees tightly to her chest.

Oliver ran his fingers through his sandy hair. "Come here. Come sit on my lap," he said at last with a sigh.

Dorrie skipped across the cold boards and climbed onto her father's lap, tucking her feet up under her long flannel nightie.

"Dorothy, once upon a time—"

"This isn't a fairy tale, is it?" interrupted Dorrie.

"No, it's a true story," said her father. "I want you to listen carefully and try to understand."

Dorrie didn't quite know why, but she didn't think she was going to like this story.

"Once upon a time, there was a beautiful girl . . ."

Perhaps it isn't such a bad story after all, thought Dorrie.

"And a stranger came along," her father continued.

"A prince," said Dorrie, giggling.

"A biologist," corrected her father. "And he fell in love with the girl. He used to see her in the meadows and in the woods. She was like one of the wild things. But he took her away from those things."

"What'd he do that for?" asked Dorrie.

"Well, he loved her. And he wanted her with him forever. So they were married and went away to the city."

"And lived happily ever after?" Dorrie guessed.

"I'm afraid not. You see, the girl . . . died. All the love in the world couldn't keep her alive."

"Mother," Dorrie murmured.

"Yes," her father replied, holding her close. "I'm trying to tell you, Dorothy, that just because your mother isn't here anymore, doesn't mean I love her any less. I can't love any other woman. Not even as good a woman as your Aunt Claire."

"But couldn't you get married anyway? You like

104

each other, and we're all so happy here," protested Dorrie.

"It wouldn't be fair. Claire deserves to have a husband who loves her as much as I love your mother."

"Like who?"

A faint smile came to her father's lips. "Well, that's for them to figure out."

"But I just thought—"

"I know. You thought it would be nice if we all lived together, happily ever after. But life isn't always like that."

"Doesn't Aunt Claire love you, though?" asked Dorrie.

"No. She likes taking care of me. That's different."

There was a brief silence. "Well, what'll happen to us?" Dorrie finally managed to ask.

"Well, first I want to tell you that I love you."

Dorrie nodded. "I love you, too."

"That's good. Now, listen: Just for a little while, I'm going to go away. Now, now," he added when Dorrie began to protest, "just for the rest of the winter."

"Why?"

"Well, for one thing, I think it's time I got out of your aunt's hair. I'm getting in the way of her life a little bit."

"But we love having you here."

"Oh, my dear, I know you do, but you must trust me, please, Dorothy. Another reason I'm going is because I need some summer sunshine."

"Summer sunshine? But where will you find it?"

"I'll go to Florida. I can be outdoors and study plants and birds, and write."

"But I thought you liked it here."

"I do, Dorothy, but, oh, sometimes the wind is so sharp, and the cold air hurts when I breathe. And I'm too . . . cooped up here."

"Like mother in the city?" Dorrie ventured.

"Yes. Yes, I think she felt like that."

"And what about me?"

"You belong here," said her father. "You feel that way about it, don't you?"

"Yes, I think so," Dorrie said. "But don't I belong with you, too?"

"Oh, Dorothy, of course you do. But I can't . . . I don't know how to take care of you alone. Not yet. I need your aunt's help. I guess she and I will share you, if you don't mind. You can live here with Aunt Claire, and in the spring I'll be back. I'm afraid," he said, "that your father is a little bit like the geese—he must go south when winter comes."

Dorrie pressed her cheek against his. "I'll miss you."

"But do you understand?" he wanted to know. "Is everything all right between us?"

"Yes, I guess so. As long as it's just winters."

"Then I think we had better go tell your aunt."

By Valentine's Day, Oliver Whitfield was packed to go.

Dorrie stood in the snowy dusk between Aunt Claire and her father as they waited on the station platform.

"I wish you'd have let me call Adam to drive. This weather is getting worse."

"Nonsense, Oliver. I'll be just fine. I've been driving these roads for years. Besides, I do just fine without any help from Adam Campbell."

They heard the whistle of the approaching train, lonely and shrill in the cold valley, and tears began to well in Dorrie's eyes.

Oliver put his arm around her, trying to comfort her. "Now, Dorothy, be brave," he pleaded, his eyes sad.

"I'm tired of being brave," she replied, half to herself.

"Good-bye, Claire," said Oliver. "And thanks."

Aunt Claire nodded. "I know, Oliver. It's all right."

He bent down and drew Dorrie into his arms. "Its not long until spring," he said.

The big train pulled in, grinding and hissing to a halt.

Oliver kissed Dorrie's forehead quickly. "I'll be back," he said, and picking up his suitcase, he handed it to the waiting conductor. At the top step, he turned and waved. "Good-bye," he called.

Dorrie's leftover tears had turned to ice on her cheeks. She wiped her eyes with a mittened hand. "Good-bye," she said. "Good-bye."

Aunt Claire and Dorrie stood there until the train pulled out of the station. It was almost dark now, and snowing harder.

"It's time to go," said Aunt Claire at last. She scraped the heavy, wet snow off the windshield and they got in the car. "I'd better not try the back way. The main road will be better. Say a prayer, Dorothy."

As they climbed the icy east hill out of Angell, the snow fell thicker, swirling heavily in front of the headlights so that Aunt Claire could barely see. "I've traveled this road all my life," she said, "but I can't for the life of me make out exactly where we are."

"We must be almost to the main road," said Dorrie.

"There's the end of Morrisons' orchards," said Aunt Claire. "And here's the corner." She turned north.

"How will we know when to turn up our hill?" Dorrie asked. "There's no orchard to see, and it's getting darker."

"Look for houses," said Aunt Claire. "Roll down the window if you have to. I have to keep my eyes on the road—what there is to see of it." She leaned forward, clenching the wheel, peering into the blinding snow.

Dorrie unrolled the window, and the wind blasted in, taking her breath away. "Sometimes I see dim lights."

"Good. Now, start looking for a row of tiny lights."

"There!" exclaimed Dorrie suddenly. She pointed ahead.

"Good," said Aunt Claire. "That's Mrs. Clark's chicken coop."

The little valley north of Clarks' was filling with snow. They went rushing through, throwing white plumes up on either side.

"The wind's from the north," said Aunt Claire. "Otherwise the road might be drifted shut. I just hope our road's still clear."

Dorrie shivered, and it wasn't just because the window was open. "What would happen if we got stuck?"

"Depends on where we were. We'd walk to the nearest house, if we could see any lights. Now start looking for another light. Tell me every time you see lights, so I can name the farms."

So Dorrie called out the lights, and Aunt Claire named the farms, until suddenly they hit a bank of snow, and the car gave a sickening lurch.

Aunt Claire gripped the steering wheel and pressed the accelerator harder. The rear wheels spun and the back part of the car slid from side to side. Then, just as suddenly, it was over, and the car was through the big drift.

"That was Crawfords'," said Aunt Claire.

"But we aren't that far yet." Dorrie was frightened now.

"The storm is worse than I'd thought," conceded Aunt Claire. "We've missed some of the lights."

"Then how do you know where we are?"

"The road always drifts across like that at Crawfords'. It's the only place like it. Quick now, or we'll miss our turn. Look for Warings' lights! And pray, Dorothy!"

"Dear God," began Dorrie. *What should I ask for?* she wondered. "Send us an angel!" Then, "There's Warings'!" she shouted.

108

"But I can't see our road," said Aunt Claire. She slowed down further from the turtle's pace at which they'd been driving. "And I don't dare stop, or I'll never get going again in this deep snow."

Dorrie interrupted. "A light!" she cried. "There's no house here. But I see a light!"

Out of the dark and the rushing snow came a steady beam that swung slowly back and forth. A signal. And then they could see the bundled figure, holding a lantern.

"It's the angel! God sent an angel!"

"It's Adam!" said Aunt Claire, turning off the main road onto their side road.

Dorrie stuck her head out the window as they approached the light. "Adam!" she shouted.

He swung the lantern in the direction of the hill. "Keep going!" he called back through the wind. "Don't stop for me or you'll never make it!"

"What's he doing out here?" asked Dorrie, drawing back into the car. "Pastor said he was sick."

Aunt Claire made no reply, but pressed again on the accelerator, trying to pick up some speed before beginning the climb up the hill.

"How can you tell where to go?" cried Dorrie.

"I can't! Roll up the window and hang on!"

The car plowed forward. Now, instead of the wind-whipped flakes, solid walls of snow intercepted the headlights' beams as the car surged through the drifts. Dorrie could feel the engine begin to grind as they started up the hill. Aunt Claire quickly shifted into low gear. Then came another drift, and another. The car was slowing, losing momentum. Suddenly it slammed into the largest drift of all, and snow billowed up around them. The car stopped.

"Are we stuck?" asked Dorrie.

Aunt Claire put the car in reverse. It wouldn't move. She urged it forward again. It didn't budge. "Not only stuck," she said, "but buried." She turned the engine and headlights off.

They sat there in the dark a minute, listening to the sounds of the storm around them. Then Aunt Claire buttoned her top coat button and retied her scarf. "Bundle up, Dorothy, we walk from here." She pushed on the door. It wouldn't open. "Try yours," she urged Dorrie. It opened a crack, but not enough for even Dorrie to squeeze through.

"What will we do?" Dorrie's voice was full of fear.

"Welcome to winter in the country, Dorothy."

Dorrie thought Aunt Claire's voice was oddly cheerful under the circumstances. "But—"

"It's all right," said Aunt Claire comfortingly. "We're close enough to walk home."

"But the car is buried and we can't get out!" protested Dorrie.

"Adam's coming. He can get us out."

Dorrie quickly unrolled the window and stuck her head out. "You're right. I see his lantern," she said. "Adam! Here we are, Adam."

Out of the clouds of blowing snow came the halo of light. *He even looks like an angel,* thought Dorrie. Then he was beside them, kicking snow aside and at last making room for the door to open just wide enough for Dorrie and Aunt Claire to slip out.

The force of the wind and the sharp sting of the driven snow took Dorrie's breath away. She gulped and turned her back to the north.

"Claire!" shouted Adam above the storm, gripping her by both shoulders. "Are you all right?"

"Yes. What about you? Matt said you were sick."

He coughed, but ignored her question. "I've been worried about you. The radio said the main roads are closing, and even the trains are shutting down before they get stranded."

"Where is daddy, then, if the trains aren't run-

110

ning?'' cried Dorrie in alarm.

"He'll be in Traverse City—he'll be just fine,'' Adam reassured her, coughing again. "Here, take this lantern.'' He thrust it into Aunt Claire's hands.

"Adam, that cough—'' she began.

"Go on ahead with Dorrie,'' he said. "If I can get the car out, I'll take it back to the corner. I hate to leave it here.''

"Adam, that's crazy—leave it!''

"I'll just give it a try. It'll be in the way of the plows. Go on, I'll see you in a bit!''

Aunt Claire turned and, grabbing Dorrie's hand, led the way up the hill.

Afterward, Dorrie could still feel the wind and snow. It had been like wading waist deep in the bay, except the water had parted for her and the snow hadn't. More than once they had fallen before reaching the warmth and safety of the house.

Aunt Claire went back out to check the cows, and Dorrie, knowing there would be no school tomorrow, sat up by the stove alone, listening to the keening of the wind, and waiting.

Half an hour went by before Aunt Claire returned. "Sorry, Dorothy,'' she said, shaking her coat and sweeping the snow from her boots. "It took longer than I thought. I strung a rope—'' Then, with the broom in mid-sweep, she stopped. A look of fear came into her eyes. "Did Adam stop by yet?''

"No,'' replied Dorrie.

"Oh, no,'' whispered Aunt Claire. "Dorothy, quick, call his house, just in case.''

Dorrie ran to the phone and cranked the one long and four short that was Adam's ring.

"But he wouldn't have gone home,'' Aunt Claire continued, half to herself. "Not without coming in first. He said, 'I'll see you.' . . .''

"There's no answer,'' said Dorrie.

Aunt Claire dropped the broom and began rebuttoning her coat. "Dorothy, get some coffee ready, and boil a kettle of water."

"Aunt Claire?" The fear was catching.

"If Adam's still out there, then something is very wrong," said Aunt Claire. Then she was gone.

Dorrie couldn't remember when she'd felt more alone. It was more than just the empty house, although that would have been enough. But her father was gone, Adam was sick and out in the storm, and now Aunt Claire had left. Dorrie said a prayer to God. It felt as empty as the house. *Please help Aunt Claire find Adam,* she asked. Inside her tightly shut eyes, she could see visions of Adam lying helplessly in the snow, perhaps even half buried like the car, and Aunt Claire bending over him. Or maybe the wind had blown a tree over on top of him and Aunt Claire was trying desperately to pull him out from under it. Maybe he was already dead. She'd read stories about frozen prospectors in Alaska. "There must be something I can do!" she cried. Then she remembered Aunt Claire's instructions. She dragged out the kettle, set it on the stove, and began filling it.

The coffee was hot and the kettle boiling when Dorrie heard the noise on the front porch. She ran to the door, throwing it open wide.

"Help me, Dorothy," gasped Aunt Claire.

Dorrie darted out, slipper-footed on the snowy porch, and ducked her body under Adam's other arm. Together they got him into the warm room, and Dorrie slammed the door shut.

"There," said Aunt Claire, as Adam leaned back against the door. "We'll get these off and get some hot coffee in you."

"Claire," Adam murmured.

As Dorrie stood watching, his body sagged, and he slid to the floor.

10
Adam's Battle

Dorrie sat curled in the corner of the sofa near Aunt Claire's bedroom. Above the howl of the wind, she could hear Adam's ragged breathing. For three days he had lain there, pale even amid the white sheets and comforters of Aunt Claire's big bed. And while the storm continued to rage outside, some strange storm raged within Adam.

Aunt Claire had called the doctor. "He can't come," she had said after hanging up. "The storm. All the roads are closed."

"But what about Adam?" Dorrie had cried.

"Doc said he was in last week with a bad chest cold. He gave him some medicine, but he figures it's gone by now."

"Then why isn't Adam better instead of worse?"

"He came out in the storm for us."

"For us," Dorrie echoed softly.

Aunt Claire nodded. "Doc says to keep him warm and give him liquids whenever he wakes up. But we can do more than that." It had been the only time in those three days that Dorrie had seen even the shadow of a smile cross Aunt Claire's face. "We know God."

Now the coughing started again, and Dorrie cringed at the sounds that came from Adam. It seemed as if his body were trying to get rid of all the breath and life inside him.

Aunt Claire hurried in from the kitchen and passed Dorrie, wringing out a wet cloth. When Adam stopped coughing, she wiped his face gently and laid the cloth across his forehead. Then she got a bowl of warm chicken broth. "Are you awake a bit now?" she called softly. "Here." She spooned in a mouthful, which Adam obediently swallowed. After the third mouthful, his eyes opened.

"Does he see you now, or is he still staring past?" asked Dorrie.

Adam made a groaning sound. His eyes were glazed with the fever. "Claire?"

Aunt Claire handed Dorrie the soup bowl and took Adam's hand. "I'm right here, Adam."

"Claire?" he said again. Then his hoarse voice grew louder. "Claire!" He struggled to sit up.

"Adam," said Aunt Claire, her hands on his shoulders, "lie down now. It's all right."

He stared at her without recognizing her. Then slowly he lay back against the pillows, turning his face to the west window. "Claire?" he whispered to the falling snow. Then he slept.

Aunt Claire came out by the stove, her hands over her eyes.

"He still doesn't know you, does he?" said Dorrie.

Aunt Claire shook her head. "No." Her voice, tender in the bedroom, was cold now. She went to the phone and rang it. "Matt, this is Claire. Matt, I need help. Have you heard when the plows are coming? No, he's no better. He still doesn't—he isn't—oh, Matt, if

you could get through . . . And bring some medicine."
Then she hung the receiver on the hook and wiped her
eyes on the hem of her apron before turning to Dorrie.

"Can he come?" Dorrie asked.

Aunt Claire nodded. "He'll try. The roads are open
one lane between Williamsburg and Angell. He's going
to try to get some medicine from the doctor and
snowshoe in from Angell."

It was getting dark when Dorrie at last saw the pastor
plodding slowly over the drifts. "He's coming!" she
called.

Aunt Claire left the stew she was stirring. "Thank
God," she said, opening the door. The light made a
path on the porch.

"I feel like a duck," said Matthew Linden, unstrap-
ping the snowshoes and coming inside. Then he took
Aunt Claire's hand. "How are you doing, Claire?" he
asked. "I hope you don't mind my telling you that you
look terrible."

Aunt Claire smiled then and hung his coat near the
stove. "I suppose I must. But I feel better now that
you've come." She poured him a cup of coffee. "Did
you get some medicine?"

Matthew shook his head. "I'm sorry, Claire. There's
only enough antibiotic for babies and old folks. The
storm, you know."

"But Adam—" began Aunt Claire.

Matthew put his hand on her arm. "Now, Claire,
he's a strong man, and Doc says as long as he keeps
coughing, he's got a good chance."

Aunt Claire turned her face away. "Strong," she
mocked bitterly. "Wait until you see him, Matthew.
He needs medication."

"Doc says you're doing as well as any nurse could."

"But I'm *not* a nurse!" Aunt Claire's eyes flashed.

"Claire," said Matthew. "You're no nurse, and I'm
no snow plow. But we don't do things in our own

strength. It's God's strength. Trust him."

She relaxed her stance and sighed. "I'm sorry. You must be tired and frozen, coming all that way, and I never even thanked you. It's just that—" She hesitated. "Matt, he doesn't know me. He stares at me like I'm a stranger."

"It'll be all right, Claire."

"You know he was out because of us. He was looking for us. It was my fault."

"Claire, don't start on that."

"Yes, of course." She sighed again.

Matthew smiled. "I see you've got a kettle of stew. You can fix me a plate while I go look in on Adam."

When the pastor came back out of the bedroom, Dorrie was waiting.

"He'll be all right, won't he?" she asked.

"No matter how it works out, it will be all right," he answered.

"Yes, but he won't—you know—die? Will he?"

The pastor sighed and put his hands on her shoulders. "Oh, Dorothy. I'd like nothing better than to tell you that nobody you love will ever die. But you know better than that, don't you?" He smoothed her dark hair.

"Yes. My mother."

He smiled. "Your mother was a beautiful woman," he said. "Not just on the outside, Dorothy."

"She's in heaven now," explained Dorrie.

"I know. We'll see her there someday." He smiled again, but not at Dorrie this time. "I'm looking forward to it."

"I know it's supposed to be very nice there and all, but I really wish Adam wouldn't have to go," Dorrie said. "Not yet. I thought everything was working out when I got to stay here, and when my father came. But lately it feels like God's not paying attention to me."

Matthew grinned. "We all feel that way sometimes,

116

but it's not true. The Bible says God's loving us and caring for us even when we don't feel it.''

"Then why did daddy have to go to Florida? And why is Adam so sick?''

"You ask some awfully tough questions,'' said Matthew. "And just because I'm a pastor doesn't mean I get special privileges from God. But I do know this: we must pray for Adam, believing God will make it all turn out right. 'And we know that all things work together for good to them that love God. . . .' ''

"Aunt Claire quotes that verse, too,'' Dorrie commented. "I'd like to believe it. I know that Adam loves God. But he doesn't go to church. Even though Aunt Claire and I ask him to.''

Matthew smiled. "I've noticed. He is a bit of a rebel. But he has what's important, Dorrie. Fellowship with God. The rest he still has to work out. And someday I believe he will. Not because we've scolded him—but because we've loved him.''

Once the roads were cleared, Doc Green came out to see Adam.

"Shouldn't he be moved?'' asked Aunt Claire.

"Where to? Home, alone?'' asked the doctor, wiggling his mustache.

"Well, no, but I thought maybe the hospital—'' said Aunt Claire.

"With all those sick people? What's the matter? You getting tired of taking care of him?'' The doctor stuck his stethoscope over Dorrie's heart. "She must have a boyfriend,'' he said to Aunt Claire. "Her heart's going *flip-flop, flip-flop.*''

Dorrie giggled.

"But he doesn't seem to be getting better,'' protested Aunt Claire.

"He isn't getting worse. He isn't dead,'' said the doctor. "Say, 'Ahhh!' '' He stuck a tongue depresser in

Dorrie's mouth. "Just as I thought. There's a dangling thing in the back of your mouth."

"Doc, really!" said Aunt Claire.

"All right, Claire," said the doctor, turning to her and patting her knee. "His lungs sound less congested, though I don't like that fever. But give it time. He's got pneumonia, not the sniffles."

"Yes, but—"

"Claire, there's nothing else anybody can do." He stuffed his stethoscope back into his worn black case. "And Claire . . . just in case anyone happens to say anything . . ."

"Gossip, you mean?" Aunt Claire laughed. "I think I'm past the point of paying any attention to gossip."

"Well, moving him *would* be harmful. If Pastor Linden stops by every few days, I'm sure that will be all that's necessary. The only person I can think of who might gossip is Ida Crawford, and she'd gossip to the spiders about the cobwebs if you put her in a broom closet." He headed for the door. "I'll be back in a day or two. Make sure he keeps coughing, and call me if there's any change."

So the vigil continued. Aunt Claire was never far from Adam's bedside, and she sat beside him, holding his hand or bathing his face while he tossed and murmured strange things.

"How can he say those things?" asked Dorrie one day from the warm room, where she was embroidering a pillow for her room.

"He's delirious," Aunt Claire explained as she straightened the sheets on Adam's bed. "The fever won't go down, and he doesn't know what he's saying—don't pay any attention."

"He sure sounds funny sometimes."

Aunt Claire sighed wearily. "I suppose so." She sank down on the edge of the bed beside Adam. Dorrie saw that there were dark circles under her red-rimmed eyes and no color to her cheeks, and even her hair had lost its brightness. "But to me it's like a scary nightmare," she continued as if talking to herself. "He can't seem to wake up from it, and I can't go to sleep."

Dorrie kept stitching, and Aunt Claire kept talking. "I keep praying about it and asking God to forgive me." She turned to Adam's sleeping form. "I know you can't hear me, Adam, but I'm so sorry, and I'd give anything in the world to make it all right again. You never should have come out in the storm looking for us that night, and now I can't even thank you or ask you to forgive me for the way I've been, the way I'm always scolding you or ignoring you while you're always so good to look after me. Adam, I simply can't stand the thought of anything happening to you. I think I would die too." She buried her face in her hands.

"Claire?" It was Adam's voice, calling again as he always did. She paid no attention, but sat huddled over, rocking herself gently to and fro.

"Claire," he said again. "I forgive you."

Dorrie looked up. Aunt Claire's hands came down from her face, and she stared at Adam. "Adam? Are you talking to me, Adam?"

Adam opened his eyes. His hand reached up and brushed the loose hair back from her wet cheeks. "Tears," he said. "For me, Claire?"

"Oh, Adam, are you all right?"

His hands took hold of her shoulders and drew her down to him. She buried her face in the hollow of his neck, and he held her and smoothed her hair while she cried to make up for all the times she hadn't.

"I'm all right, Claire," he whispered. "Everything's going to be all right."

Adam gazed out the window at the rain falling on the honeycombed snow. He was sitting up in bed, the coverlet cluttered with books and farm catalogs. "What

119

time is it?'' he asked.

"Four o-clock," said Aunt Claire from the bedside rocker.

"I just got home from school," said Dorrie. "You know what time that is." She had her homework spread on the dresser top.

"No, I don't mean time of day," said Adam.

"Friday, you mean?" asked Dorrie.

"Year," said Adam.

"Time of year?" asked Aunt Claire, dropping her mending and staring at him.

"It's raining out, the snow looks old, and are those crocuses over by the shed?"

"Oh, my goodness, I never thought to tell you, and you haven't been well enough to ask. You missed winter," said Aunt Claire. "It's the end of March."

"I've missed winter." Adam laid back against the pillows.

"Well, I wouldn't look so sad," said Aunt Claire, resuming her mending.

"You mean I've missed all the snow storms and icy roads and power lines down and school closed?"

Dorrie abandoned her papers and hopped up on the bed beside him. "Oh, Adam, you're not serious."

"You let me sleep through the winter," he admonished Dorrie.

"You hibernated, just like a bear. We tried to wake you up."

"And I wouldn't?"

"No. You just talked funny."

"Oh," said Adam. "Tell me, what did I say?"

"Dorothy," interrupted Aunt Claire, "how about running into—"

"Hold on now," said Adam. "You're the ones talking funny." He turned to Aunt Claire. "How come you don't want her telling me what I said? After all, I said it, so I have a right to know."

"Well, it might be a bit embarrassing," said Aunt Claire.

"Yeah," said Dorrie. "Mushy stuff like love and all that."

"Oh," said Adam slowly. "Mushy stuff, huh?"

"Dorothy!" Aunt Claire's eyes flashed their warning signals; her face turned red.

Adam ignored her. "Well, now, Dorrie, tell me. Who was I saying all this mushy stuff to?"

"Aunt Claire."

"Adam, please don't encourage—"

"Now, now, Claire," said Adam, reaching out to pat her. "Better you than, oh, Miss Ida, for instance."

"Adam, honestly!" exclaimed Aunt Claire.

"Well, what I want to know next is, what did Aunt Claire say back?" continued Adam.

"Oh, Adam," said Dorrie. "You weren't really talking to Aunt Claire. Oh, you were talking to her—but you didn't know she was there."

A strange look came over Adam's face. "I what?"

Aunt Claire looked up slowly, her eyes meeting Adam's. "You didn't know us. You were delirious. You talked to me, but you were in another world. You couldn't get out, and I couldn't get in. For days."

"Days?" Adam was stunned for a few moments. "Now, tell me this," he said at last, leaning close to Dorrie and whispering. "What exactly did I say to your Aunt Claire—the mushy stuff? You know."

"Well," said Dorrie, taking a deep breath and then plunging in, "you told her you love her."

"Ahhh," sighed Adam, lying back against the pillows once more. "I was afraid of that. My deepest secret." He turned and gazed at Aunt Claire, whose bright head was bent over her work. "It's been a well-kept secret for years. It took total delirium for me to part with it."

"Aunt Claire kind of cried," volunteered Dorrie.

Adam's eyes never left Aunt Claire. "You cried?" he asked. "You didn't throw old shoes at me or anything?"

"No," she retorted, not looking up. "You were too sick."

"Look at me," he said.

She raised her head, her eyes wet.

Adam reached his hand out to her, and she put her hand in his.

As March gave way to April, Adam grew restless. "Time I was outside," he said. "My apple trees never got pruned. How can you expect me to have a good crop this year when you've kept me locked up in this house away from my orchards?"

"Doc said you could be up, but not outside. Besides, you know very well that the Warings pruned your trees," said Aunt Claire.

"It's not the same," grumbled Adam.

"This may come as a shock," said Aunt Claire, "but your orchards can survive without you."

"The whole world is a bedroom," Adam went on, throwing up his hands in mock despair. "Dorrie, is it fair? Your aunt keeps me imprisoned here. It's torture day after day!"

"Torture?" Dorrie laughed.

Adam rolled his eyes. "Oh, Dorrie, you don't know what it's like. She makes me take naps whether I'm tired or not, and when she does let me up, I have to sit with my arms out like this to hold her yarn, and then she makes me lift my feet up so she can mop the floor."

"Oh, Adam!" laughed Dorrie.

"But that's not the worst. There's more."

"Adam, stop this nonsense," begged Aunt Claire.

"She refuses to answer me when I ask her questions," Adam went on.

"What's the question?" asked Dorrie. "Maybe I

know the answer.''

''Go set the table, Dorothy,'' said Aunt Claire firmly.

Reluctantly Dorrie left them and went to the kitchen.
She thought about how happy she was to have Adam
almost better again. It had been frightening while he
was sick, as if her whole world was on the brink of some
dangerous edge, ready to fall and crash into a million
pieces. Now her world was safe again. So why did she
still have this funny feeling, as if something didn't
quite fit?

She thought of Adam and Aunt Claire in the other
room. When she was away from them, even now, setting the table, she missed them, but they went on
without her. And then she realized that the something
that didn't quite fit was herself. *I belong to this house
now,* she said to herself, *but I don't belong to what
Aunt Claire and Adam share.*

When the table was set, she slipped back into the
warm room and sat quietly by the stove, not wanting to
disturb the voices in the bedroom.

''You shouldn't tease her like that,'' Aunt Claire was
saying.

''I'm not teasing her. I'm simply courting you.''

Aunt Claire laughed softly. ''Courting me?''

''Well, it is a bit difficult, lying flat on my back in
your house week after week! Probably takes some of the
romance out of it. When did Doc say I could go out?''

''End of the week, if it's nice. Don't be so
impatient.''

''It's not impatience, Claire, it's longing. I haven't
the strength to be impatient.''

''I wish I could make you stronger,'' said Aunt
Claire.

''You can.''

''How?''

''Marry me.''

Dorrie, by the stove, felt her heart beat faster. She was sure now that she wasn't meant to be listening to this, but if she moved, they might hear her and stop talking, and Dorrie didn't want them to stop. Besides, she wanted to hear Aunt Claire's answer.

"Before, I always lost my temper and patience and walked away because I couldn't stand to stay around as the loser," said Adam. "Now I'm too weak to walk out even if I wanted to. I'm done with walking out. And you're done with denying me, Claire. You *will* marry me. I'm not asking anymore. I'm telling you—because it's the only way for us."

"Oh, Adam," said Aunt Claire. "I don't know what to say."

"Well, that's something new. How about saying yes!" he said. "You do love me. I'm not mistaken about that, I'm sure."

"I do love you, Adam."

"Then why haven't you been saying so? And when I say I want to marry you, why aren't you falling into my arms?" And then before Aunt Claire had a chance to answer, he rushed on. "Oh, the church, it's the church, isn't it? But it's all right, Claire, because I'm coming back!"

"But you can't just come because you want me to marry you. It's got to mean something to you," Aunt Claire protested.

"First you want me to go, and I won't, and now when I say I will, you tell me it's not for the right reason. And I haven't even told you the reason."

"Well, tell me."

"It started with Dorrie."

"Dorothy?" echoed Aunt Claire.

"She got me thinking, ever since last summer. All the things I said against the church, about the hypocrites and the mirror worshippers. I said some hard things, Claire, you know me. And Dorrie just blew her

124

nose and told me she loved me.''

"Oh, Adam.''

"Well, I can't let it be like that any longer. Those people I accused of being hypocrites—Claire, I am one of them. Because I haven't been loving and accepting them any more than they did me. Dorrie said something about letting God's love shine through us. And God loves those people; he accepts them. So why can't I?''

"Oh, Adam,'' said Aunt Claire again.

"Please say something more than 'Oh, Adam,' '' said Adam. "Why won't you say yes?''

Aunt Claire laughed and sniffed at the same time. "It's Dorothy,'' she said at last.

"I don't understand,'' said Adam.

But Dorrie understood. *They don't want me now,* she thought. *They'll want babies of their own and I'm no baby.* She buried her face in her arms to muffle the sobs she felt welling up inside her. She almost didn't hear Aunt Claire's answer.

"I love you dearly, Adam. But I couldn't marry you if it meant giving up Dorothy.''

Dorrie raised her head and caught her breath.

"Giving up Dorrie?'' echoed Adam.

"Don't ask me to, Adam. I've been so foolish. But now that I have her, well, I couldn't stand to give her up.''

"But, Claire—'' began Adam.

"No, please, just listen. I have to tell you. You see, when we were children I thought it would be so simple. You would marry Margaret, and Matt would marry me. It was childish, I know.''

"But Matt didn't—and I—''

"I know,'' said Aunt Claire softly. "Matt didn't love me at all. It was Margaret he cared for. And it was you who loved me all the time, wasn't it, Adam.''

"Yes,'' he replied. "All the time.''

"But I was too foolish, too envious to see it. First I lost Matt—though I never had him—and you went off to the war while I was still moping. The folks went so quickly the next winter. And then I lost my Margaret. When she died . . ." Aunt Claire paused. "I wouldn't take Dorothy then. You didn't know that, did you? Oliver asked me before he entered the sanitarium."

"But why did you say no?" asked Adam.

"Because I didn't want to love her and then have her taken away. I knew she couldn't be mine."

"You weren't thinking of her, letting her go to those old aunts."

"No. I was thinking of me. But now that she's here for good—Adam, I couldn't ever give her up!"

"Why should you have to?"

"I was afraid—I thought you might only want—"

"Claire, did you ever give me a chance to tell you what I wanted? Did you think I wouldn't want her, didn't love her?"

"But that's different from having her as your own."

"Claire, listen. I wouldn't ever ask you to marry me if I thought it would mean giving up Dorrie. She's part of the marriage offer. I can never claim the love she gives to Oliver, but the rest of her is mine," he said fiercely. "Ours."

"Are you sure?"

"Am I sure?" he said loudly. "Dorrie!"

Dorrie silently tiptoed back to the kitchen door so they wouldn't know she'd been listening. "Yes, Adam?"

"Dorrie, do you love me?" he hollered.

"Yes, Adam, I love you."

"Is it all right with you if we all get married and live happily every after?"

Suddenly the warm feeling of belonging rushed in. "Oh, yes, Adam!" Dorrie cried. And she ran to the bedroom.

126

11
Naming

The circle was completed. It was May again. The apple trees had tight pink buds almost ready to swell open, the calves were being born, and Dorrie had been at the farm a full year.

"You're late for breakfast," Dorrie called to Adam as he climbed out of his pickup. She sat on the porch waiting for Aunt Claire to finish getting ready for church.

"But right on time for church," Adam replied, coming up the steps.

"Are you coming with us, then?" she asked.

"No, you are coming with me."

Dorrie flung her arms around him, and Adam laughed, hugging her.

"Look, Dorrie," he said. "Remember last summer, when I said those things about church?"

She nodded.

"Well, I'm sorry. I said the people weren't loving, but I wasn't loving them either. I was a hypocrite. Dorrie, I don't want it to be that way for you. I want you to grow up accepting, loving people, because being a Christian isn't something you just think about by yourself in the fields. It's actions, too. And if I don't take you to church, if I don't show love, then I can't very well ask it of you, or anyone else. It has to start with me, do you understand?"

Dorrie looked up into his eyes and nodded once more.

"It's too busy," said Aunt Claire on the way to church. "Calves coming, and the garden needing to be planted, and Oliver expected any day."

"You forgot something," said Adam.

"Well, that's what I mean," said Aunt Claire. "We'll practically have to sandwich the wedding in between Bluebell's new calf and the string beans!"

"Can I name the calf?" asked Dorrie.

"Yes," said Aunt Claire. "I just hope you pick something with a little more personality than 'Calfie'!"

"I'll get the garden in this week," said Adam. "Dorrie can help me after school while you finish the dresses, Claire."

"Oh, dear, the dresses!"

"Now, what's wrong?" asked Adam.

"Well, don't you see, that's just one more thing!"

"Claire, I've never seen you so upset by work before."

"Well, I suppose maybe I'm a bit nervous," she admitted.

"I thought the groom was the one to get nervous," said Adam.

At church, he parked under the elms and held the pickup door for Aunt Claire and Dorrie. Then he left them and went around to the side of the church and in the basement door.

"Isn't he coming in with us?" asked Dorrie.

"No," said Aunt Claire, as they climbed the front steps.

"But I thought he was really coming to church with us."

"He is. But he's doing it his way. Wait and see." Aunt Claire smiled.

As the congregation rose to sing the opening hymn, the double doors at the back were flung open wide and the choir filed in. And there, walking in the sunlight, head thrown back, mouth open in song, came Adam. As he passed by their pew, he winked at Dorrie and grinned, and she could hear his big voice singing out the joyous words:

> I sing because I'm happy,
> I sing because I'm free.
> For His eye is on the sparrow,
> And I know He watches me.

During the service, Pastor Linden announced the forthcoming marriage. "And Claire and Adam have asked me to say that all of you are invited."

After church, Miss Ida Crawford came bubbling up. "Why, Adam Campbell," she gushed. "What a divine voice. It's been years since we've heard you sing, and when I heard you this morning, why, I felt just like a sparrow myself!"

Dorrie thought Miss Ida would make a rather large sparrow.

"And, Claire-dear, what thrilling news!" Miss Ida went on. "I was just saying to Mrs. Clark, 'Now, don't they make a divine couple!' If only Pastor Linden would find someone." Her eyes were mournful for a moment, and she sighed.

"I'm sure you could work on that, now that Claire and I are taken care of," suggested Adam. "Someone with your obvious talent . . ."

Miss Ida's face lit up like the sun. "Do you think so? Well, let me see, I've heard there'll be a new teacher coming in the fall. . . ."

"Adam, how could you?" said Aunt Claire after Miss Ida had left.

"Why not?" he laughed. "She's said 'What a divine couple' to you with three different men this past year. Time for her to concentrate her energies on someone else for a change."

They shook hands with Matthew Linden at the door.

"Not long now," said Matthew.

"Well, depends on how much time Claire has left over for weddings, what with gardening and calving and all." Adam winked at Dorrie, and Matthew laughed.

"By the way," said Matthew. "After all the excitement dies down, you're all invited over to visit David and me."

"David?" exclaimed Dorrie.

"Soon as school's out, he'll be up here for the summer. In fact, he should be here in time for the wedding. I'm moving my things into Will and Halley's little cottage next week. Guess the new French teacher is going to rent Mrs. Clark's room next fall."

"Say, about that teacher—just be on the alert," said Adam.

"How's that?"

"Well, it seems that Miss Ida Crawford—"

"Oh, no," groaned Matthew.

"I'm afraid so," confirmed Adam.

"Heaven help me," sighed Matthew. Then he laughed. "Well, who knows? Maybe she'll be a raving beauty, and I can brush up on my French and recite sonnets to her by the chicken coop!"

Each day brought changes. Dorrie had picked out pink rosebuds and intertwining blue ribbons for her new wallpaper, and now the room was ready for the fresh white curtains. Adam painted the outside of the house, and although Dorrie missed the familiar gray boards for a while, she had to admit the clean white siding was an improvement.

Aunt Claire had taken special care with her bedroom redecorating. "I know you've spent hours staring at these walls," she told Adam. "I want it to look like a whole new bedroom."

"Claire, could I ask just one favor?"

"Why, of course!"

"No pink rosebuds? Leave those to Dorrie."

So Aunt Claire picked a cream-colored wallpaper with chocolate sprigs on it, and she hung cream-colored curtains. And when it was done, Adam stood in the doorway and scratched his head. "Are you sure it's the same place?" he asked. He looked at the new quilt on the bed, a patchwork of browns and russets and ivory and pale gold. "Where'd that come from? It looks good enough to eat. Like hot chocolate with cream and honey pouring in."

"It's our wedding gift from the Ladies Aid," explained Aunt Claire.

"Ladies Aid, eh? And Miss Ida is president. I should have known it would look like food."

Oliver arrived by train, looking tanned and much stronger. He had several crates and boxes with him. "Been to the mangroves and the Everglades," he explained when they met him at the station at Angell. Dorrie couldn't wait to help him unpack.

"We're fixing Adam's place up for you, daddy. So you'll have lots of room for your collections and things."

"Sounds wonderful," he said, his brown eyes gazing at her. "Maybe you'd like to spend some time at the bay with me this summer, looking for Petoskey stones?"

"Oh, could I?"

"In between gardening and milking," he promised.

So the wedding drew nearer, and at last the apple trees were in full bloom, and the last pieces of lace trim

131

had been lovingly stitched, and the last pair of fresh curtains had been hung. The garden was in except for the tomatoes, cabbages, and peppers.

And Bluebell had her calf. "I'm going to name her Edelweiss," Dorrie announced.

"What?" gasped Aunt Claire.

"Edelweiss," repeated Dorrie. "It's a Swiss flower. I read it in my geography book at school."

"Fine name," said Adam.

Of course the sun was shining on the wedding day. It shone through the stained glass window more brilliantly than Dorrie had ever seen it before, making the shepherd radiant and alive.

All the ladies cried a little afterwards and examined the wedding dress and the gold ring, and all the men poked their elbows into one another's ribs and felt awkward all dressed up on a Saturday afternoon. And all the children ran circles around the cake and punch tables, and Adam asked if there were any cucumber sandwiches or sardines to be had.

Dorrie greeted David shyly but soon he was telling her about a good spot to fish under the willows, and she was explaining about Bluebell and the calf.

When it was time for Aunt Claire and Adam to leave for their honeymoon site, a cottage with a rowboat over on the bay, Aunt Claire called Dorrie to them and hugged her. "You take good care of your daddy, and we'll be home soon. Don't forget that Mr. Waring will be up to do the chores, and Miss Ida's going to bring in your suppers. And don't forget we love you, Dorrie."

"Dorrie?" echoed Dorrie, looking up. It was the first time Aunt Claire had ever used that name for her.

Aunt Claire smiled. "Yes. You're my Dorrie now—our Dorrie."

And Dorrie glowed. *Like stained glass,* she told herself, thinking of all the love.